Praise for *The Man in the Ban*

"*The Man in the Banana Trees* kicks ass. Every story is a surprise. The dexterity of Marguerite Sheffer's prose is absolutely awe-inspiring. By turns heartbreaking and brilliant, Sheffer's stories remind one of George Saunders and Amy Hempel in their playfulness and through their special eye for tragedy."—Jamil Jan Kochai, judge, Iowa Short Fiction Award

"*The Man in the Banana Trees* is a truly remarkable work of literary art and marks the arrival of an absolutely brilliant new storyteller. Marguerite Sheffer is an endlessly inventive writer, but she's also a philosopher capable of drawing metaphor and meaning from the lives of ordinary people trapped in extraordinary circumstances. Following the path of acclaimed writers like Borges, Márquez, Link, Machado, and Keegan, Sheffer promises to provide remarkable stories for many years to come." —Maurice Carlos Ruffin, author, *The American Daughters*

"A collection that writes its own miraculous language for the meaning of art and the question of our moral obligation to others. The range here dazzles—a contemporary ballet stage, a nineteenth-century artists' colony, a ship full of ghosts, a life stalked by grief in the form of a virtual-reality tiger—and all these pictures are knit into a single breathtaking view by a sensibility that's both empathetic and unyieldingly keen. *The Man in the Banana Trees* is a blaze of light, brilliant enough to illuminate not only its characters' interior lives but also the reader's own."—Clare Beams, author, *The Garden*

"Rarely have I come across ideas as original, prose as exquisite, and hearts as bared on the page as those found in this collection. I am blown away by its achievement. Marguerite Sheffer is extraordinary."—Julia Phillips, author, *Bear*

"Haunting and hilarious, horrifying and heartwarming, this is short story gold. Marguerite Sheffer is the alchemist, reimagining and transmuting the form." —John Vercher, author, *Devil is Fine*

"*The Man in the Banana Trees* is magnificent. Marguerite Sheffer entrances with stories that are strange, unexpected, and full of imaginative magic. These stories are unbound by time, leaping from a romantically and intellectually entangled trio of researchers in 1960s England who discover the first pulsars to a commodore in purgatory, forced to view his descendants from the belly of his ship. By slanting our reality, Sheffer's stories ask us to glance anew at our world. Brimming with life, love, loss, and longing." —Crystal Hana Kim, author, *The Stone Home*

The Man in the Banana Trees

Iowa Short Fiction Award

The Man in the Banana Trees

Marguerite Sheffer

University of Iowa Press · Iowa City

University of Iowa Press, Iowa City 52242
Copyright © 2024 by Marguerite Sheffer
uipress.uiowa.edu
Printed in the United States of America

Cover design by Erin Kirk
Text design and typesetting by Sara T. Sauers
Printed on acid-free paper

Library of Congress Cataloging-in-Publication Data
Names: Sheffer, Marguerite, 1987– author.
Title: The Man in the Banana Trees / Marguerite Sheffer.
Other titles: Man in the Banana Tree (Compilation)
Description: Iowa City: University of Iowa Press, 2024. |
Series: Iowa Short Fiction Award
Identifiers: LCCN 2024010253 (print) |
    LCCN 2024010254 (ebook) |
    ISBN 9781609389956 (paperback; acid-free paper) |
    ISBN 9781609389963 (ebook)
Subjects: LCGFT: Short stories.
Classification: LCC PS3619.H451454 M36 2024 (print) |
    LCC PS3619.H451454 (ebook) |
    DDC 813/.6—dc23/eng/20240402
LC record available at https://lccn.loc.gov/2024010253
LC ebook record available at https://lccn.loc.gov/2024010254

For all the students and teachers I have had
the honor of working with

It is not your duty to finish the work,

but neither are you free to neglect it.

—PIRKEI AVOT 2:16

Contents

Rickey

"RICKEY NEEDS a break. Can you come get him?"

The text comes from Odell in the bio classroom. I grab my lanyard and my walkie-talkie; I take the stairs. I go to perp walk Rickey to the Reflection Room, again.

When I get there Odell seems to have regained control. The ninth graders, in their ripped jeans, are rotating from lab station to lab station, setting up wet slides and adjusting microscope platforms. I spot Rickey's felt-and-feather form. He is in the corner, deposited on the teacher's rolly chair, with the big broad desk separating him from the other children.

We never had a puppet student before Rickey. He is sitting on his gloved hands, maybe to keep himself still. His fuchsia felt torso is breathless. He spins silently in the chair. The paler pink feathers around his neck flounce.

"That's five more pipettes," Odell whispers. I clock the sparkling glass remains in the plastic bin on his desk. I nod. I am here to help. I wonder if there are other schools that would be more supportive learning environments for Rickey. I don't think we can keep this up.

We call them "outbursts" and invent terminology to express our acceptance and patience. We assign him to Tiered Support Services, write him a 504 Behavioral Plan, and grant him a "health exemption" from swimming. Some of the faculty assume he is mocking them when his felt eyelids stretch way back, his eyes full circles of awe, as he learns something new. Sensitivity training helped them with that, to a degree. In staff meetings, we remind ourselves: he doesn't mean any harm. But we are already making so many accommodations. At lunch he picks up a special tray piled with the wax fruits and vegetables from a child's play kitchen.

Every student deserves an education, deserves to thrive. I believe this. But no student can be allowed to interrupt the schooling of their peers, and that's where I come in.

I crouch down next to Rickey, who is engulfed by the chair. Now he is swinging his stick-thin blue velvet legs and his puppy monster paws. He doesn't want to look at me at first; he considers the windows. We've had this conversation many times before. I fear I'm just following the empathy script now: get down on the child's level, lead with questions, lay out clear next steps.

"Rickey, come with me for a minute."

He ruffles and turns to me. As I kneel next to him, up close I can see the scratches on his ping-pong eyeballs. I'll need to remind the other boys about that. They don't mean anything by it. It is tricky, I know; Rickey enjoys the rough play. His body can take a beating. He invented a game where the others throw him through things: alley-oop him over the bathroom stalls or into a dumpster or out of the open second-floor window, once. He loves the slapstick; he can be bashed and tossed and emerge unscathed—theatrically sailing like a kickball with his limbs trailing limply behind. He pops back up; he laughs. Yet, he is vulnerable to the littlest pricks and snags: scissors, sharp corners, fingernails even. These little marks sink in and stay sunk; he doesn't bleed or bruise, but the rips in his felt won't just mend themselves. His sparkles come away on our hands, and we wash them down the schoolhouse drain with stubborn pink industrial soap.

At my request, Rickey hunches his shoulders, hangs his head, and plop-hops down from the rolly chair. I sigh; so dramatic. He shuffles his large fluffy feet against the linoleum. The other kids stop their chatter to watch. They get distracted by his perpetual performance. That's the root of the whole issue. Rickey loves class, but too much. He sucks up all the air, all the attention. The other ninth graders give Rickey a covert little wave before they return to their pond scum. They have adopted Rickey as a kind of mascot; I worry this is an unhealthy attachment. They validate Rickey's behavior, which is the last thing he needs. I've seen some kids start to imitate him, maybe unconsciously, speaking in his exaggerated singsong cadence.

It is just the two of us in the hallway, and I guide Rickey toward the Reflection Room, though it's not like he needs directions. Rickey and I have spent many hours there together. We are a progressive school; the Reflection Room has a painting of a butterfly on the door, a thrift store couch, acrylic paints, and a lamp I brought from home to soften the light. Rickey made the garlands that decorate the room himself, those colorful chains of interlocking circles that are really a more appropriate project for younger students.

Yet Rickey does not want to come with me. He slows his steps and swivels his head to and fro.

"Tell me what happened," I say. I'm holding his hand, which I wouldn't do for the other ninth graders, but he likes it. His hand is soft and the exact temperature of the air.

Last time, it was singing during the state exams; the time before that, gnawing playfully on his classmates' hair and fingers; another time, doing elaborate jigs during Silent Sustained Reading—his reading level is the highest in the grade, so we know that's not the issue. Perhaps a combo processing and attention disorder.

"Did you know that euglena have both plant and animal characteristics? They have their own *chloroplasts*, and also a *tail*. They *hunt*, too." Rickey gives me this knowledge like a gift. At least he was paying attention in class. Perhaps he relates to the euglena, not quite this and not quite that. "How much sand do you think it would take to bury me? Or what about you?" Rickey asks.

"A whole lot," I answer, to keep him moving.

Worse, once during Spanish groupwork, Señora Garfield heard shrieking and found Rickey sitting in the center of his assigned cultural research project team (Guatemala), pulling back the fabric of his midsection to show the students what lies underneath. Later, we rationalized: he forgets the others aren't built like him, how shocking it can be for them. That day, though, Señora Garfield told us how Rickey was laughing with his mouth wide-open in joy as he used his nubby hands to pull back the curtain on the vacancy inside him: *nada, nada*, just air, popsicle-stick scaffolding, and some seams of hot-glue. He apologized the next Monday in front of the whole class. He said he thought they'd like to see.

Of course, the other kids in his group were pretty shaken, and of course, it got around the whole school. Sophomore Shirley Abramson came in for counseling, saying sometimes she suspected, sometimes she was so *sure* that she was full of emptiness, too. She had thought it was just her, till Rickey went around showing everyone. Now she was less alone. Now she could not ignore it.

I try again. "Why," I ask Rickey when we are walking in parallel, "are we here?"

"We are here to learn," Rickey answers. He swings my hand in his. He has already forgotten to be sullen. He is looking all around with curiosity, though this is the same hall he walks every day.

We pass a poster that just says YET in big green letters. *Yet*, I think, *we are all working too hard to keep having this conversation; Rickey is not progressing as he should.* There are other students who need our attention, too. I'm thinking we should put him on a discipline contract, maybe try different incentives. Something needs to give. This situation is good for no one. I'll speak to the principal about alternative placements: perhaps a school with a no-nonsense approach, or one that is arts-enriched.

A senior, Andie, walks by, huffing under the weight of her backpack, wearing her world weariness like a coat from the wrong era, all the buttons and seams and buckles just slightly off. When he sees her, Rickey ignores my questioning and waves to her. He drops my hand and scuffles over to her. He comes up to her knees. The senior's face inflates with joy.

"What do you like in your tacos?" Rickey asks.

I learn that Andie's favorite filling is sweet potato. She must be running late for something, some class or appointment, but doesn't seem hurried anymore.

Watching them, I don't think they are particular friends even, but in that instant there is a sense that the two of them might just, any second now, shed their bookbags, abandon the building, and walk through the hilly woods. They might continue, pointing out the insects, the birds, the fungus, the names of colors, pausing to read every historical marker and plaque—an odd, impromptu traveling pair—till they get to the train station, its vibrant map, and then emerge and join the raucous chorus of the city. Or maybe they will go to the shore and take turns burying each other in sand.

This is what happens so often in Rickey's classes. As if he rips a skylight into the popcorn ceiling. And the sky distracts from the lesson plan. There's a reason we have roofs.

"Rickey," I say, seriously and low. He walks away from Andie and joins me, reaching up to grasp my hand again.

The Reflection Room is in sight now. Beyond the door, Rickey can sit alone and pick from a jar of colored gel pens and some blank paper to write letters of anger or apology. Then, maybe, after enough time and contrition, he will be allowed back to class. Some students like the

Reflection Room so much they try to sneak in here, to stay. But not Rickey. He tries to be penitent, to earn his way out. He writes eloquent long apologies filled with figurative language; he regrets saying and doing the wrong thing; he wants to be better; he does not understand what he is doing wrong.

That means, I know, that he is not listening, for I've told him many times what he is doing wrong. I've told him to look at his peers, see how they are, try mimicking them. Don't reinvent everything. Don't show off. Don't stand up from your desk and walk to the windows when your favorite garbage truck goes by. That the teachers have his best interests at heart, and their directions will be his guide. That I am here to help, but I can't do it for him.

We walk through the especially quiet of an empty school hallway that will soon be echoing with sneaker squeaks and children's shouts.

"Miss, I need—"

Ricky seems to slow. He is apprehensive about his consequences. His hand drags in mine.

"Consequences are part of learning, and I know you love learning," I tell him. I keep pulling. He must go. I am already behind.

"Miss . . ." Rickey's voice sounds soft and distant.

"Rickey, let's get a move on."

I am walking along holding Rickey's hand and then two things happen at once: I hear a slight collapse—the falling of something very soft to the floor—and Rickey's hand goes loose in mine.

Looking back I see—strung out across the long hallway—all the pieces of him. I do not see what snag Rickey has gotten caught on, but I have been pulling. In frustration, I tugged too hard, noticed too little.

Soundlessly and quickly I scramble to the floor, hands and knees. Andie is on her hands and knees too. There are little bits of glitter stuck to my hands, I see, as I wave her away. She shouldn't see this. She is gripping her laminated hall pass so hard she might slice herself open. She is bending over to pick up some of the trim that was once Rickey's shoulder. She is calling for help, but there is only me.

I crawl to gather all the pieces of Rickey before the bell rings. I worry he will be trod underfoot, scattered, before the other kids even see.

I reach for the limp sequined fabric, the ping-pong balls, the empty gloves, the popsicle sticks, the twine that acted as a pulley for Rickey's elbows, knees, and wrists. Loose feathers float across the linoleum floor. I grasp at them.

I can only hold so much at once. One of the balls that were his eyes goes bouncing away, down a stairwell.

I try to make a cradle out of my lap, sitting on the floor. I press my fistfuls together, willing them to stick, to reconnect, to move, to flex and shimmy and shiver. But when I pull my hands apart, his materials fall through and down. The feathers drift the slowest and land on top of the pile—soft, still, and finally silent in my waiting lap.

The Unicorn in Captivity

1493

The tapestries are worth more than the walls. For feast days they are hauled out and hung, adding life to the cold stone hall. Eight panels depict the capture of the unicorn: the hunters, in the end, victorious— bright red threads.

When the tapestries hang, it is like the young queen's wedding all over again. Then, they still stank of vinegary dyes; their threads were gleaming, overlooking hens, puddings, and hot wine.

Now the trumpets of battle blare; the castle is under siege. The young queen thinks, *The unicorn is me: treasured, trapped but able to see beyond its flimsy cage.*

She steals away to a place no one will recognize her. She leaves the tapestries hanging, to slow the conquerors, to distract them with treasure. The barbarians behead her husband. The world ends.

But she survives a little while longer, a handful of years. She finds work at a mill. She covers her hair with a white kerchief. The world goes on.

1789

The chateau is a riot of torches and pillaging and shouting and stomping. The common folk rip down all the grandeur, every sign of obscene wealth. The marquis's fine ceramics mosaic the floor.

Many rough hands pull down the tapestries. They might extract the metal from the gilt threads, like they do the gold teeth from the rolling heads, the aristocrats giving back—finally, giving in spite of themselves.

But a cobbler, seeing the unicorn tied up in that little man-made fence, so slight, thinks, *We will display the tapestry as our flag so everyone will see: our brotherhood is the unicorn, the aristocracy is the fence, and the whole future of liberty is laid out like a green carpet to sink our hooves into.* The cobbler calls on his brothers-in-arms to carry the tapestry out before setting the whole chateau alight.

The cobbler sees the guillotine himself, soon afterward.

1843

The tapestry is a blanket. It rests in a barn in northern France. Sweet and oily fingers touch it often, for there are many children there. In a hard freeze it warms root vegetables.

A favorite cow gives birth under it. The calf has a white mark on its forehead where a horn would be. The family pampers her and calls her Licorne. They give her ribbon crowns and the sweetest sounding bell for her neck. The calf nuzzles into the stiff folds of the tapestry. She softens them with rolling and gnawing.

After two unyielding years of famine, the family abandons the farm. They leave Licorne in the yard and the tapestry in the barn. Now a cow, Licorne lies on it and misses the family, wonders why they have left and what she is to do now.

Tufts of her soft brown fur become permanently woven into the weft of the tapestry. They will not be able to be removed, later, without causing damage.

2043

The museum warden is standing on a ladder propped against a stone wall. He is loosening the tapestry panel from the sturdy clips that hold it up for viewing. He is cradling it gently to the floor as it falls. He is too old for this shit.

On previous nights, the warden would watch the tapestry shift in the slightest of breezes, as if alive. Now he wrestles it like a body, like a gentle giant. The warden has spent years alone at night with the tapestry, with the unicorn, wondering why the beast doesn't make a break for it. He decides that what he is doing now, crouching his old knees carefully beside its old threads and starting to roll, is a kind of guarding too.

The warden hears the rest of Manhattan beyond the oasis of this museum—a helicopter, a siren, the rip of a military jet. Are those regular city sounds? Or warnings? After the president's broadcast, he is hyperaware. Probably everybody is. It is unclear: Should he continue to go to work? Is the subway still safe? For how long?

The warden has hired an outrageously priced cab to drive him two miles to where the Little Red Lighthouse touches the Hudson. This is where he has arranged the drop-off. He watches the river and waits for bubbles. What surfaces is white, the size of a van, beaching itself lightly. It beeps. A hatch opens.

It is tempting, of course, to throw himself in, to straddle the tapestry, to ride it all out. He's heard others have tried. But these are vacuum submarines, not built for humans at all.

He only had room to send one panel of the tapestry, so he chose the one reproduced on tote bags—his favorite and everyone else's: the punch line to the eight-panel comic strip, "The Unicorn Is in Captivity and No Longer Dead." Sure there's an arrow; sure there's a chain around its neck and a paltry fence. But it lives.

2073

All that green, the children of the sunken city think. They press their greasy hands against the plexiglass that protects the tapestry. A familiar material to them; it keeps the water at bay. At least a little while longer.

They are more fascinated by all the green than the unicorn—that seems less plausible. They've seen plants, of course, but also behind plexiglass, in little rows. They've learned the name of the color but never seen it as the backdrop to everything. The interpretive materials share that the tapestry once doubled as a botany textbook: 101 different species of foliage portrayed. Can you find them all?

"Why doesn't the unicorn just break free?" one asks.

Her question is not answered on the plaque.

"Use your imagination. For all we know," her teacher replies, "he might."

At the Moment of Condensation

CareCorp seeks information regarding the person(s) who interfered with the moisture collection facility of Precipitation Catch Basin 31 on the afternoon of Friday, April 24.

Diversion of atmospheric moisture, commonly called "rain theft," is a felony and will be dealt with to the fullest extent of the law. According to Oklahoma State Law (1.3.XXIV), any such moisture becomes the property of CareCorp at the moment of condensation, when such condensation occurs in corporately owned airspace. CareCorp has invested heavily in localized cloud-seeding and rain-harvesting efforts in order to provide stable hydration resources to our community. Personal harvesting or hoarding of this precious shared resource is illegal, even in small amounts. Removal of water from the free market's economic cycle harms us *all*.

To aid the public in the identification of the miscreant(s), CareCorp has disclosed the following details:

At 4:13 p.m. on April 24, seventy-six drones assembled above Precipitation Catch Basin 31 at an altitude of roughly 2,500 feet, hovering between cumulonimbus clouds (altitude: 4,200 feet) and the Care-Corp catch basin. Drones were of the recreational type available at mass-market stores. Attached to the underside of each drone was a single inverted umbrella. Enhanced security video shows the umbrellas were secured to drones using household materials, including twine, ribbon, and shoelaces.

Several distinct umbrellas were observed:
· Translucent pink umbrella with "cat ears"
· Yellow umbrella illustrated with ducks in galoshes
· Child's umbrella with pale lavender and blue ribbons attached to tips

If you recognize these umbrellas or believe you may have seen similarly flagrant umbrellas on the street or in private domiciles, please come forward.

CareCorp loss prevention investigators believe that perpetrators are utilizing umbrellas saved in personal storage for the last five to eight years of sustained drought. Be aware that those involved are likely to be between thirteen and nineteen years of age, an assumption based on the childish nature of several umbrellas and the rarity of new umbrellas in today's marketplace.

Evidence obtained from security footage suggests the involvement of multiple such individuals in a highly coordinated operation. As rainfall ceased, drones gathered briefly in close proximity to form a colorful three-dimensional teardrop or raindrop shape. At this time, corporate espionage or hostility is NOT suspected, due to the haphazard construction of the drone vehicles and the frugal nature of involved supplies.

Security forces pursued the vehicles until they exited CareCorp airspace and scattered in various directions simultaneously.

Though the water-carrying capacity of each craft was small, resulting losses to the corporation over the approximately twenty-five-minute period total over $8,500 in expected revenue. Such violations will not be allowed to continue. Penalties will be sought in an effort to deter copycat criminals. If unresolved, CareCorp will be forced to increase water prices by up to 25 percent for the next rain cycle.

We at CareCorp pride ourselves on our stewardship of this valuable resource. We appreciate your help living up to CareCorp's mission to "PROTECT, SERVE, and RELIABLY SUPPLY" the populace. Those with knowledge of this incident are encouraged to come forward by contacting their community's CareCorp liaison. We entreat the public to aid in our call for justice.

The Observer's Cage

SHOW ME THAT picture again. How *marvelous*. Of all the photos, this one made it into a textbook. This must be from '67. The discovery gets, what, a paragraph? A line? But I can see why they chose to include the picture. It's a good one. I'd forgotten about it, but I remember the day. Lizzie's smile is genuine. It looks like someone said her name and she is lifting her head from reading the telescope's radio printouts, and you can almost see what was written on the pages on her face. *Beaming*, that's a fitting word. Emitting; caught between the telescope and the world of the living.

She loved being the first to know. To have a great secret to unleash upon us all. That hunched posture, maybe not the most flattering but accurate. She was often like that, hunched over printouts and readings and dials. Quite a revealing photo: see how Ernest is just behind her, has already adopted a grand pose, has thrown a hand on her shoulder? That's them.

. . .

I did? Well, that makes sense now why I'm not in it, if I was the photographer. I'd forgotten.

. . .

Thank you for humoring an old man like me. I'll try to remember. It makes sense that most of your questions are about Lizzie. I'm glad she will be getting the prize. Very well deserved. Too late, though, isn't it?

. . .

I had come to stay with them, Lizzie and Ernie, at the ugliest house in England, a little cinder block cabin that skirted the edge of the telescope's field. Just the three of us and some sheep, situated only an hour or so away from Cambridge. I rarely left. We had too much to do. Each day, the telescope generated hundreds of feet of paper, of data. The long scroll sprawled across the table, spilled onto the floor, pooling and curling.

The cabin was owned by the university, as was the meadow, but it was ours alone for those two years. Funny how so short a span, so long ago, can be the hinge you swing open on, like an enormous door.

At first I had the pullout couch. There were always dishes in the sink. The cabin was made of modern, austere materials: concrete blocks and high narrow windows. The opposite of Cambridge and its stone arches. It pushed us often to the outside, even when it was cold. To smoke and look out at the telescope.

Don't imagine a disk; don't imagine a chalice embracing the sky. Instead imagine a grotesque grid of wire and sticks. Like a labyrinth made of fencing, always listening. The posts kept the wires up and out of the moisture of the grasses, at an elevation of about five feet. You see, the telescope ran on radio, so the grid was cast over a wide area of the countryside. A big net to catch radio waves. The Four-Acre Telescope, we called it.

. . .

There's a telescope in the States, in California, that I visited much later. Palomar, in San Diego. One of the last great reflector telescopes, a glorious two-hundred-inch mirror. I went there mostly to pay homage: that sort was the kind of majestic telescope we had doomed into oblivion, even though ours looked like a county science fair project in comparison to Palomar's grand barrel and dome. By then I hadn't spoken to Ernie or Lizzie in, what, twenty years?

I visited Palomar during proper night. I was given the insider's tour by a fellow astronomer; they let me sit in the observer's cage for a spell. I climbed a ladder into the elevated chamber near the machinery of the telescope.

"Back in twenty," he said. Then he closed me in. I was suspended in a tube. My only companion was the telescope. You become essentially a human component of the device, devoted to its care and interpretation, dwarfed by it. Some compare it to a prison. I had to wait for someone else to let me out.

That's how our ugly cabin seemed sometimes: an odd observer's cage for our odd telescope. Bare, isolated, close-quartered, a little wondrous; we were just watchers, together. Floating apart.

I remember us laughing at some shared joke over a meager meal of what we called bachelor's pasta: al dente spaghetti with a pat of salted butter to melt onto the noodles, and a can of whatever was handy— Heinz tinned vegetable salad, turnips, or wet peas—on top of that.

No, I can't remember the joke. Only Lizzie slapping my knee and saying, "Don't you dare." There were only proper dining chairs for two, so one of us, a rotating third, was always seated in the cushioned plaid lounger pulled up oddly to the table. It wasn't the right height; from it, you couldn't quite reach the light or the meal or the utensils or the wine. You were forced to sit back and watch, like dinner theater.

I imagine from the outside the cabin must have looked like a beacon, alone in the wide dark field, blaring light and music out of the small windows. We'd play records and dance and sing the lyrics loudly and badly late into the night. We had no neighbors.

· · ·

I had met them, both of them, at a beginning-of-the-semester party at Cambridge in 1964. I had wanted to impress Ernie, as I wanted to be pulled into his research group as a postdoc. I was carefully sober and sharply dressed and attempting to be very clever. Lizzie—Elizabeth— was introduced to me as a "faculty wife." I know. Ludicrous, now. The telescope was her design, though based on Ernie's research.

It was en vogue to play Motown at these parties, at least that year. The Ronettes. I remember because Lizzie, afterward, at the cabin, was always humming something doo-wop-y to herself under her breath while at work in the meadow or at the little receiver desk.

They were married before they came to Cambridge, so yes, Lizzie was the faculty wife, but she was also an unfunded, unacknowledged research partner. She'd never have gotten the position on her own, that wasn't an option back then. There were some women, later, in the seventies, among our postgraduates, but only a few. I often suspected Lizzie had married Ernie to get into the group. She never denied this when I'd accused her.

"Wouldn't you have done the same?" she'd asked.

"Oh, I'd have done much worse," I said back to her naughtily.

"Worse than marriage? Hardly!" Her laugh felt like a dare.

· · ·

It was not glamorous work, not like their rooms at Cambridge, which were filled with books, with freshly bound reports and graph paper and the smell and smudge of graphite pencils, little colored dregs of liquor lining the bottom of heavy glass tumblers left out on the veneered side tables from the night before.

Rather, everything in the cabin was vinyl, slippery, used by the previous tenants. There was the constant impression the two of them had been up all night talking and working. I romanticized their tiredness, the sleep in the corners of their eyes, the glamour of Lizzie's curls that were oddly bent by falling asleep in her chair with her head sideways against the cushion. Some nights I put them to bed, carrying Lizzie, Ernie leaning heavy against my side, my shoulder, my chin, his touch a heavy electric line, not unlike the wires that made our telescope. Apt to tangle. "Gorgeous when she is asleep," Ernie said to me. Lizzie didn't hear.

· · ·

In the early years the funding streamed in—Cold War cash for the strongest radio receivers possible. The service was mad about the idea. They had only a vague idea of how the telescope worked, of what was possible. But they liked Ernie's clean haircut, his pressed jacket, his shoulders. His reassurances. The novelty of the technology. They left us alone mostly, but would phone in nonsensical requests every odd month. They'd had reports of a covert Soviet submarine operation near Antarctica: "Can it hear that?"

"No, it cannot"—there was an entire dense planet between Antarctica and the telescope. That kind of thing. For that reason, when we first caught the signal, we kept it to ourselves. We had no idea what it was, what it meant.

· · ·

When she found it, Ernie was off on a speaking tour of German universities, so the maintenance and minding of the telescope was left to Lizzie and myself. It was a galoshes-and-cocoa affair.

Part of my job, as junior researcher, was to untangle the sheep when they got caught in the field of wires. When a sheep ran afoul of the telescope, it was as if a parcel of the sky vanished, dead, emitted no more warm fuzzy radiation. Ernie joked that we might hear a heartbeat "if the beast were to crucify itself just right."

· · ·

I knew something was odd because she stopped her humming. She held the cushions of the headphones against her ears. She sucked in on her cigarette and then forgot to let it go. She coughed. The smoke and sound burst out of her into the room.

· · ·

Set the scene? I remember there were fruit flies in the summer, in the cabin. *Bastard flies.* I poured bleach down the sink to try to outroot them, but still they came. They made little living halos around our glasses of sherry. Accusatory. I led the campaign against them; Lizzie could not be bothered, and Ernie was so often away. What worked best as a trap was a drop of dish soap in a cup of cider vinegar, or in more of the wine. The soap breaks the surface tension of the liquid so that the fly cannot find purchase and sinks into its favorite drink. They'd float there, but none of the other flies saw that as a warning.

Poor Ernie, he came back one late night from some university in Belgium to find the front room empty. He must have been parched and the lights must have been low, because he tossed back a glass of that horrid mixture. We both awoke to his sputtering. Lizzie figured out first what must have happened; she sat up in the sheets and started laughing. I left to help Ernie.

You can ask, it's alright. We'd been in bed together. It was not a secret. Well, it was, but not from Ernie. Ha. If anything, he'd ask to watch, if not join in.

Ernie was paranoid. He said they'd cut our funding if they found out what went on between the three of us. Of course he was probably right.

I'm glad things are easier now, for people like me, people like us. I hope they are.

· · ·

I've always wondered how other people avoid falling in love all the time, with everyone they meet. I think perhaps they are not watching closely enough.

If you are a touch ugly, as I was—all knobby knees and Adam's apple and thin hair perpetually outgrowing its conservative cut—you are more likely, perhaps, to be watchful. To catch the little gestures, like when Ernie turned Lizzie's wrist over and over to the rhythm of an American song, the way you might make a dog's paw dance, while she read *Nature*. He was the best dancer of the three of us. Lizzie was always slow by a beat; Lizzie, who went soft in his arms, as if he could infuse her with grace. She was small; it was a surprise how bossy she could be.

In the morning before it got too hot, Lizzie would be out in the meadow maintaining the lines of the telescope, her hair up in curlers under a plastic yellow bonnet. Sometimes she'd change for dinner. It might be just a fresh, clean sweater, but her *hair* would be glamorous. Curled. She had a bit of camp about her. Another reason we got along. Both of us performed our roles. Fighting over Ernie's attention and then comforting each other when he was absent: he was often absent, often at work or off otherwise.

"Funny that work is being *away* from the telescope," I remember Lizzie would remark. Of all of us, she was the most tied to the telescope. It had been her idea. "All these men and their obsession with disk size. A thirty-foot disk, a sixty-foot disk, a hundred-foot disk." Part of her genius was to imagine a different shape: the wide fragile net.

· · ·

Of course. They say if you rolled out all the nerves in the body end to end, they would go for miles. The telescope was like that. A field of wires, nerves, 120 miles laid out in a grid, back and forth and back and forth, sensing, listening, receiving.

I'd call out positions and frequencies while she'd record, then we would switch.

Lizzie knew the telescope intimately. She had nicknames for the nodes that most often failed and required the most attention. Her "fussy dozen." I think she liked them more for their noncompliance, for their constant need to be untangled and tightened and set taut.

Lizzie preferred it out in the meadow with the wires, even in the bad weather. A badge of courage. Only an astronomer would be found there, she seemed to insist, not an astronomer's wife. I played her assistant, though technically I was part of the lab and she was ancillary. Perhaps that's why the two of them chose me for the project, at least at first: my willingness to defer to Lizzie, to submit to her authority.

· · ·

As I said, in the end Lizzie heard it first. As was so often the case, Ernie was away, so she shared it with me. We huddled around the receiver. For a moment we were the only two people on the planet, the only two of our species to share a secret clue about a thing very far away, about the nature of the very elements. Can a church wedding hold a candle to that?

· · ·

Is it strange that she did not wear makeup when Ernie was out? Is it strange that I did? We felt rascally and wild, egging each other on. The shade of her lipstick that looked best on me was aubergine. My eyelashes have always been naturally long, longer than hers, with the effect on my slim face and frame of making me look rather like a tall, lanky fawn. I'm sure this all seems tame to you now.

It seemed tame then, is what I am trying to tell you. There was no audience to be scandalized, except for one another. It was just us and our insatiable curiosities. Ernie would blush when we teased him about such things, then he'd put his hand on my trouser, my thigh, and Lizzie would egg him further. "Don't you dare." He liked being teased, we liked teasing.

I'm trying to say that out there in the cabin it was as much drag for Lizzie as for me when she put on a dress, some eyeliner, her blush.

· · ·

Ernie? Ernie was able to do the work of two astronomers because of her. He was in two places at once, able to be out promoting the project while the telescope was well minded. You have to remember that this may be an extreme case, but it was common back then. Every man we knew was twice as accomplished as they'd any right to be.

He wasn't a villain. I think of him as boyish, despite being the definite head of our little household. We were possessive about him. After all, he was both of our tickets, his attention like a lantern. We feared what would happen if it waned.

My father had dogs like that, like us, once. When he was with them, they were testy and jealous of each other, ears and tails up, baring teeth and knocking each other in the skull to get to his hands. When he was away, they could not be apart and slept in one bed.

Ernie was good at people, the kind of man my father was glad I was working under, as if that would straighten me out. Ha.

He'd write little dirty jokes in the margins of the printouts before I would analyze them. He'd pass me a sheaf of papers, saying, "Have a look at these, won't you? Something curious in there."

Inevitably I'd end up red-faced when I found his penciled handwriting. Even though no one was around to see. His words were pushed in, so even when I erased them, the indent remained. When the experiment ended, all those papers were folded and stacked and boxed and sent away to the university. I wonder if they are sitting in some archive somewhere.

Ernie'd watch to see if I'd betray some subtle reaction. I'd shuffle the volatile pages back into the stack, still smoldering, like a magician's ace. He'd chuckle from across the room at his own desk.

Later he'd come up behind me when I was washing the dishes— Lizzie probably occupied with the field or the receiver—and press my hip bones into the cheap linoleum counter so hard that they bruised.

He could be surprisingly tender, too. Soft, like a barely browned apple, a side he showed only the two of us. When I was down with a bad fever, it was he who soaked a wash towel in chilled water and draped it over my brow. I must have looked atrocious. He bent over me, mirroring my delirious expressions. When my frown relaxed, his did too. He put his hand on my chest, silent, till I fell asleep.

When I woke up, I could hear the two of them bickering a room over in the small kitchen. Pacing and whispering sharp, sudden words I couldn't make out. Honestly I found it comforting, having them so near, even their arguments. One of them—Ernie, I suspect—had used a book, Hoyle's *Nature of the Universe*, to prop open the window and give me a breeze.

He was very devoted to Lizzie. He isn't to blame in this. He didn't design the world that couldn't recognize her accomplishments; but neither could he imagine a different world, a better one.

• • •

I doubt after all this time ... well, I'd appreciate it if you ran it by Ernie first. Play him these recordings, will you? I'd like to know what he thinks. Is he still of sound—?

No, no, not for years. We've never talked about it. Not then, not now. I wasn't sworn to secrecy or anything like that. The world has changed so much in the intervening years. Will you play this for him? I'd be curious to see what he says.

I used to follow his achievements in the news, but it has been a long time since he's been mentioned. It seems strange to be such old men; it never stops being an alien idea. I don't like to imagine him that way. His youth was part of him, as much as his intellect and his shyness and his hunger.

Play him this and see what he says. Maybe he'll let you share it, or part of it. Maybe he will deny it. Maybe it will make him remember.

Will you play it for him?

• • •

Yes—right. A regular, strong, distant thrumming coming from the Crab Nebula. It did sound almost alive. Lizzie pushed her headphones deeper into her skull.

At first we called the discovery a bit of scruff. A bit of faff. In case it was nothing.

. . .

We went through many notions of what it might be. We looked for terrestrial causes first. I went out to try to clear the lines, but they were clean, clear, empty, waiting. Eerily still in the morning sun.

We considered a fault in the equipment. Or the Soviets, of course. I called around to the local authorities to see if anything strange had been reported, any beams of light or weather phenomena. We checked the papers. Nothing conclusive. Meanwhile the thing just went on; Lizzie never stopped listening. It must have been maddening for her. The beat going on and on and on. The printouts flickering.

The pulse was undeniable and steady, if unexplained. Stupendous, in the oldest sense of the word—of being unfathomably large and incomprehensible, uninterpretable. Though that was in theory what we were set to do: to make sense of it.

. . .

"Pulsating source of radio" was what we put in the paper. There wasn't a name for them yet, of course. The regularity of the radio blasts was in itself an irregularity. Nothing like it had been heard before. One hundred fifty beats a minute.

I was glad it was Lizzie who found it. We'd been looking for something else entirely. But, when you start listening, you can be surprised by what you hear.

. . .

Ernie came back two nights after we'd started tracking the pulse. Seeing our faces, he dropped his bags right by the door and came over to the monitor.

"No! Really?" he said. His bags stayed in that spot for what felt like weeks afterward. He clapped Lizzie on the shoulder. He picked her up and spun her around; her shoe fell off. She was grinning but practically scrambling to get back to the headphones already. I know she must have loved him because instead of putting them back on her own head, she pulled the headphones over to him, uncoiling the heavy gray cord. She studied his face as he frowned, listening.

You could tell Ernie was a bit hurt, to have missed it. In his absence we'd already moved beyond his early misconceptions and enthusiasms.

"No, it moves, turns as the night sky turns, so it cannot be local to the solar system."

"No, the frequency remains stable over time, so far at least."

"One hundred fifty beats per minute."

"It doesn't appear to contain any sort of message, except, perhaps, 'I am here; I exist.'"

Ernie suggested extraterrestrials, and though that had been our first thought, too—little green men beating a great cosmic drum millions and millions of miles away—there was no real reason to suspect that was the source of the sound.

Ernie pursed his lips and resigned to listen as we described the moment Lizzie had first heard it, interrupting ourselves to laugh, remembering how we stumbled around and clutched at each other. "You see, we had feared it might disappear, might only exist for a moment."

But it kept on thrumming.

It was like dipping your fingers into something really eternal and sprinkling it on yourself, a blessing, a momentary reminder of the vastness of the cosmos. Like the cool basin Catholics have at the entrance to their dark cathedrals. Holy water.

Ernie sat with the telescope and donned the headphones often after that. He annotated his own set of printouts, he compiled tables and figures, but he could never enter the moment of discovery. The seal was already broken.

· · ·

Lizzie would return, often, to listen to the sound. When she walked by, she would hook the silver headphones with one finger and nest them in her curls before even sitting down at the receiving desk, before reaching for the corresponding printouts. Even when it was my shift, she might sometimes, passing by, pluck the headphones off my head, or lift just one cup from my ear so she could nestle in momentarily, side to my shoulder, ear to nose, her nostril breath fogging up my glasses. We'd hold very still. Like a single animal; a fox catching the electric scent of a distant thunderstorm. She'd hear the beat, confirm it was still going, and then go back to the relentless, tireless maintenance of her fragile telescope made of such humble materials: sticks and wires.

· · ·

The paper listed only the two of us: Ernie and me. You'd like me to tell you she was outraged? She was not. She got back to work. She said she was glad: she wouldn't have to lose time to present the paper, to manage the edits, to receive the awards, to write recommendations, to shoehorn her feet into heels. In retrospect, sure, we'd all like her to have been a vanguard for her sex, to have rallied and accused, to have made a righteous stink. But that is not the woman I knew. She cared little for the world of men.

If she was frustrated, she didn't tell us. Maybe—I've never considered this before—maybe she didn't think us worthy of telling.

· · ·

People are drawn to pulsars; people call them "lighthouse" stars, which is very accurate. The "pulse" is more accurately a beam of energy sweeping out from the poles of a quickly spinning star, like that of a great lighthouse. The "pulse" is us being caught in the light.

· · ·

I accompanied Lizzie to the doctor. We didn't correct the nurses who assumed I was her husband. When they used the ultrasound machine on her stomach, it was as if she'd swallowed the thing, the signal, by all that incessant listening. We looked at each other quickly; I knew she was thinking the same thing. It was miraculous.

It didn't last, though. There was to be no child.

It didn't last, but it did speed the deterioration of our unconventional arrangement.

Suddenly, they wanted privacy; their door was often closed to me. "Give us a bit," they said. They didn't specify what the bit was. *Time*, maybe, or *distance*. The child might have been mine, but they thought the grief was all theirs.

· · ·

Lizzie's discovery was part of a reckoning, a reframing of the way we speak about the universe. The violent universe they call it now; the view that the cosmos is not cold and perfect and orderly but warm, hot, violently hot, full of bodies tugging on each other—full of collisions and divisions.

· · ·

I'll grant she was openly livid about the end of the project. After the discovery went public, there was talk of the Nobel. Ernie was offered a position at a prestigious Australian university. There was nothing she could do but follow. She had no credentials of her own to continue the work alone, and it had always been the property of Cambridge even so: the cabin, the receiver, the posts, the wires, the field. She slammed the front door of the cabin with such force that she dared you to follow her. She walked out among the wires for a time, alone, till it got dark.

There wasn't some dramatic parting, not one moment I can point to. Just a gradual cooling, the decline of their attentions. There was an understanding that the two of them were leaving for Australia and that I was not invited.

They began to confide in each other again, without me. They were still fighting but neither came to me anymore after their rows. We somehow lost each other in that three-room cabin.

We had to train the new crew on how to use the telescope; the cabin would be theirs. Ernie and Lizzie left the task to me, as junior researcher. I was surrounded by their boxes and their rubbish—the things they couldn't be bothered with.

The flies persisted; they'd come back in the heat. I showed the new recruits how to loop the paper in the printer so it came out clean and unwrinkled. I tightened the loose wires. I bent on the floor and scrubbed for the first time in two years. Layers of grime. I wiped us clean.

When I went back to Cambridge that fall, every bench seemed empty, every hallway full of people who were suddenly younger and less interesting, less real than we were. I didn't stay long myself.

• • •

At first I felt taken. A victim of their voracity, their wanting to be loved, each wanting to get more than they gave, and me a willing worshipper at the altar of their marriage. They wanted their marriage more because I wanted in. They wanted each other more because I wanted them. They wanted to control the drawbridge, and they did: they pulled it up.

• • •

The signal is still there, of course. For years afterward I'd point toward the Crab Nebula and listen. From Cambridge, from California, from anyplace. We've identified thousands of other pulsars, but none with that exact frequency. It won't go on forever, but it is going on, still.

Now I find it rather pretty, the thought that the bodies of the cosmos are not orbiting in perfect regular solitude, like was once thought. Rather, they are exerting their gravity on one another; they are left a wreck by each other. Some of the most beautiful nebulae appear to me as great bruises, where star systems have collided and bent each other into marvelous patterns of color and light. Lizzie would say I am being "poetical," by which she means dramatic, by which she means sentimental, which to her was a form of blindness.

Despite all the jealousy and frustration, I think of them warmly now.

You can drown in love; I'm sure that's not a novel notion, but it was new to me, to be allowed to. To be allowed in the secret rooms, at least for a while. To have no part of me kept apart and hidden.

There was one more happy evening, before we all left the cabin for good. We stepped outside into the night and tried to catch sight of the

Crab Nebula with our bare eyes—a long while sitting very dark and quiet and still and all looking together, becoming just sense, sensation. It is a dim thing, but it is there, if you keep looking and waiting. Of course we ended up hearing and sensing each other too, reaching for each other even if we didn't mean to. Ernie's hand on Lizzie's. Lizzie tugging on my scarf in a rhythm, her brows furrowed.

Ernie saying, "Darling, do you see that?" and none of us sure who he meant.

In a way, I've spent the remainder of my life trying to get back to that cabin: the small, drab outpost where the universe seemed vast, vast and wild enough to embrace all of us, all of me.

Yellow Ball Python

LAMINATED EIGHT-and-a-half-by-eleven posters on every telephone pole in a three-block radius announced that our neighbors had lost their yellow ball python. We stopped to read the signs while the dog tugged and pissed. Black text on a white background—no snake photos, just a sun emoji to lighten the mood. Sunny was LOVED and LOST, also SKITTISH, but FRIENDLY, NOT DANGEROUS, and NONVENOMOUS.

TEXT IF FOUND. DO NOT TRY TO HANDLE.

Soon after, we started the chain of jokes. One of us stepped out for a jog: "Watch out for yellow ball pythons!" Opening a car door. Of course, the ceiling vents. Climbing the ladder to the attic to pull down orange-and-purple Halloween lights. Opening grocery bags, backpacks, loads of laundry. Pointing out nonsensical things on the road to Costco, neither yellow nor slinky enough to be the missing snake.

"I think I see it, there, the yellow ball python."

"No, that's just a blue tarp python."

"Oh, my mistake."

It got more absurd. Anyplace a python might fit, then anyplace they couldn't. In the oven; in an email.

"I'll show you my yellow ball python."

"Oh yeah?"

Peeking in each other's ears, like bushy-eyebrowed magic uncles who extract gold coins. In every mundane task, a yellow snake lurked; one rumored to be kind, but still a snake, after all, with fangs.

In a porta-potty before an early a.m. road race, I envisioned the python curled in the basin below me, waiting to unleash its nonvenomous bite. I told you and you laughed and then we ran.

"Stay vigilant."

You beat my time. I watched you pull farther and farther ahead.

· · ·

We ran out of places it might be hiding. Or our imaginations weren't up to it. The joke got old, got stale.

"I get it. Can we be serious? Please?"

"You used to be fun."

The laminated signs came down. I liked to think Sunny made it home; you thought his former family just gave up looking.

I googled couples therapists. We'd settled into our routines so fast—too fast. We'd only been living together for eight months. I felt absurd.

Was this surrender? Or was it surrender not to try?

· · ·

I found him after we hadn't spoken in a few weeks. You were still paying half the rent—so level-headed, so kind. We were working out a custody agreement for the dog.

It was one of those warm red nights when everything feels like it is thrashing; the kind of atmosphere that must get sailors worried, or delighted—one or the other, I can never recall. I almost missed it. A flash of yellow in my peripheral vision—under a bush in the parking lot of our Chipotle. A buttery coil. It was muscular. It was bracingly alive, trying to hold itself still but flexing just a little; thick, scaly, and gleaming. The python's spade head was pressed into its curves, to cower or to strike.

It looked back at me. It did not appear to be dying of hunger. Maybe someone was bringing it burrito bowls.

I imagined reaching for it, avoiding the eerie jaws. They were closed now, but I knew they could yawn open, swallow me whole. How do people hold pythons, heavy and strange, without spilling them? Without hurting them, or getting bit? You should have been with me, within arm's reach, looking over my shoulder. Then I might have been braver. The space where you were not, maybe that's where all the evening's electricity was coming from.

I stayed still. The python was rotating its coils in that alien way, not actually moving, just motioning within its territory, repositioning, preparing, all potential energy. It might strike; it might flee; it might stay.

I took a step back. I took a photo to send to you.

We'd agreed to take a cooling off period, but surely this was a reason to break our reasonable, self-imposed rules. I'd won! I'd found it, the real thing. You were the only person on earth who would get it completely, who might celebrate with me.

But on my phone, it looked rubber, so fake that you might think I'd planted it there.

Off the border of the screen, the python was dappled with light in its hiding place. Probably it wanted nothing to do with us, just wanted to eat rodents and roam parking lots and slither, belly low, menacing exposed ankles, shedding dead skin to be always new, freshly stamped. The yellow ball python belonged in the equatorial grasslands, but against all odds, it was thriving in the suburbs, unconcerned and uncontained.

I deleted the photo. I walked away. I didn't want proof. I didn't want the game to end; I didn't want to stop looking for improbable pythons in the piping of our everyday lives, for this wild thing between us. I didn't want you to stop looking.

The Midden

IRIS HAD DONE well for herself and so wanted to invest in some land: something reliable and permanent, a sound investment. She'd saved for eighteen years; she cashed out her 401(k). After months of site visits, she had found the most charming plot of land in the city. She was sure of it. Unlike her mother, she refused to second-guess things.

This was her lot. It was in the right neighborhood; the oak trees made for uproarious shade. The overgrown yard was skinny and long: a rarity in her historical city. The agent said its potential was endless. Iris could build a house here that was perfectly her own. She might even add a pool, someday. By then, there might be children to swim in it, a partner to play lifeguard.

Iris took her mother out to a nice lunch to celebrate. The milestone felt realer with a witness, and her mother was the perfect—perhaps the only—person who could recognize how far Iris had come. Iris wanted to involve her mother and enjoyed introducing her to the kind of fashionable and new places she would never go on her own, like an act of charity, or education.

They sat outside, the white tablecloth lifting in the breeze, and ate chargrilled oysters, meaty and slippery. Between bits of conversation, they lifted the jagged saline shells to their lips. The only sour note, Iris thought, was that her mother kept apologizing needlessly: for arriving early, for changing the subject, for asking too many questions. Iris snapped at her for it but couldn't well apologize herself, then.

Their sidewalk table skirted the intersection where angry SUVs routed around an abandoned roadworks project. Her mother was more interested in this hole than the blue-crab hummus. She kept glancing over there while Iris described open floor plans and trends in patio design.

Iris's mother had been a minor archaeologist for a stint. In her twenties, she'd spent summers in Delaware excavating three-hundred-year-old outhouses for clues about ancient diets and diseases. She spoke of those times often, like those summers belonged to a different person: a plucky, impossibly young one, who subsisted on tuna straight from the can and drove a Chevy that constantly broke down.

While Iris was paying, her mother wandered over in her pale sneakers and khakis to the edge of the rectangular cutout in the pavement, barriered only by thin tape and orange cones. She lifted the tape to get closer. Iris went to remind her of their next appointment—bathroom fixtures—but for a moment stood beside her looking down at the exposed cobblestone, surprisingly fresh: an older road preserved below. Her mother brushed the hair from her eyes, said, "Baby, would you look at that."

It was this minor detour that inspired Iris to consider offering her mother the chance to conduct the dig on her new property. The city required one before building could begin, in order to assess the site and rule out the kinds of burial-ground bludgeoning that made for unpleasant headlines. Iris figured her mother would enjoy this project. Her retirement seemed empty. Besides, she'd know the best way to conclude the dig without delay.

Weeks later, Iris propositioned her mother while they were sifting through salvaged stained glass. Iris had long imagined a venetian glass window over the kitchen sink: her model image torn from *Southern Living* and moved from rental to rental.

"Shouldn't be too big a project," she ventured. "I'd consider it a favor."

. . .

Iris visited her land on the first day of the dig. Her mother was holding a clipboard and directing the men in English, then thanking them in Spanish. "Gracias, gracias." Iris had wanted to make introductions but soon felt out of place. She tried to imagine the soaking tub she'd picked residing in its new spot, but it was a struggle amid the noise.

"Did you find anything?" Iris asked her mother that night on the phone.

"Mostly today was setup."

"Oh. Do you expect to find anything?"

"Oh yes. Always something."

. . .

The next day two workers were digging in a chessboard pattern marked out by string.

"Glass bottles." Her mother pointed her to a growing pile. "From old drugstores."

"Can I touch them?"

"From around 1810! Aren't they remarkable?"

Iris would not have gone so far as that. The bottles were heavy and caked in dirt, but might otherwise have been used yesterday. They were empty, but holding one, Iris imagined cool cola thickening under the earth into a pungent syrup.

· · ·

Two weeks later, Iris was selecting counter slabs, running her manicured fingertips over slices of geologic time—sandstone, limestone, the imprint of reeds and small spiraled shells; pressure and fissure—thinking, *This one will go very nicely with the brass faucet*, when she got the call from her mother.

"A significant discovery"—her mother breathed hard—"a midden."

· · ·

Arriving, Iris saw that the orderly string squares were mapping out a deeper and widening tear in the ground. The birds of paradise she had hoped to save had been uprooted and flattened by the excited feet and wheelbarrows of workers hauling away clay. A seawater smell had emerged, repulsing her future neighbors, who paused in the street to murmur complaints.

"Why, it could be another World Heritage Site," Iris's mother was saying. She was arguing on the phone with a representative from the neighborhood association.

Iris recalled fourth-grade class field trips to prominent local middens. Her mother had chaperoned, extolling the mysteries of these mounds: essentially very old Indigenous trash heaps, pottery and banks of oyster shells tossed aside after eating, piling up into the high ground beneath them, their great accumulation providing safety from floods and signifying ancient settlement. "People! People were here!" Iris's mother had insisted. She'd taken dozens of photos, which, when developed, seemed to Iris to show little but dirt.

Iris listened as her mother paced. "600 BCE . . . a time of peace. For so long we've conflated civilization with edifice . . ." Her eyes were shiny, unequivocal, holding no hint of apology.

· · ·

Everyone soon lawyered up as the significance of the site—two-thousand-year-old cooking ash, stone tools, ceremonial objects—became clear, and the dig dragged on. There were cold and long silences. Arguments between Iris's legal team and the parish's took place on letterhead: debates over valid ownership and appropriate compensation for the home's assessed value and the sideswept renovation. Numbers went up and down, back and forth. Iris drove with her phone in her lap but did not call her mother.

Eventually, Iris gave up her fight for the property. She forfeited her claim to her lot upon learning that her mother was planning to testify for eminent domain on the side of the parish and the state and the memory of the long gone Tchefuncte: testify to the irreplaceable archaeological significance of this upturned ground. Iris's dreams for the house began to feel small in comparison, and she folded them back in the box of herself.

She signed copier-warm papers on the top floor of a sleek downtown building with floor-to-ceiling windows, the word *settle* heavy in her mouth.

· · ·

But Iris's surrender was seeded months before the settlement, on the night she brought takeout to the dig site. There were still weeks to go before the authenticators and experts would be called in. It was late at night, and Iris knew her mother had not eaten. She found her in the open pit. Flood lights illuminated the dirt like the surface of a moon.

Iris passed her mother's muddied hands an iced tea and a plastic-wrapped utensil pack. There was the pleasant snap of Styrofoam tabs. Brushes attuned to the tasks of unearthing, from brutal bristles to soft dusters, lay around her mother. Iris had never seen her so at ease.

They sat together on the edge of the hole, legs dangling over. They forked sweet plantains.

"Let me show you something," said Iris's mother. She offered the handle of a filthy trowel, gripping the sharp part in her own hand.

Iris accepted it. They dropped together into the clay.

Iris dirtied her knees.

"Come see, baby." Her mother palmed the rough earth, so Iris understood she was allowed. Iris dug the trowel in. She plucked an oyster shell from the warm walls that embraced them. It was ruffled, then smooth. Something familiar, though the living flesh of the oyster was long gone. In that hollow, Iris glimpsed what her mother saw in the midden: the traces of a thousand too-brief lives. Each shell was another peal of laughter echoing in a just-vacated room; the jokers and the joke were lost to time, but their laughs lingered, innumerable. They were never hers at all.

How We Became Forest Creatures

I FOLLOWED JUST behind my sister Ada, near the back of our herd, single file, holding tight to the piss-yellow ribbon. My hooves dug softly into the undergrowth. Ada carried her four young on her back. I didn't have young of my own, as yet, so they were as my own to my heart. The littlest, Simon, swayed limply as she walked, asleep. Children are too stupid to be afraid of the forest. Still, I hated to see mothers shushing them. Well in front of Ada, at the front of our line, the eldest led; one who remembered the exact tree trunks marking the only safe path. The rest of us held fast to the piss-yellow ribbon and followed.

We were far from our proper home. Most days we graze the plain—the green sweet tips of swaying grasses under hoof, tickling our snouts, the green scent baking off heady in the hazy air. By the end of each season, we have bared the plain, and must make our way to the next and let the previous reseed and grow wild in our absence. It is a rhythm, us and the green plains and the dark forest between.

The forest should terrify us. In the forest we are hunted. The forest has the sweetest food of all, nectarous hanging fruits and sour pulpy fruits, and there the ungrazed grasses grow to be as tall as our heads, but we never harvest there because in those grasses and in the shadows of the trees are ferocious beasts that seek to eat us without contest or care.

They came out to watch us parade, looming on the edges. On one side, the chompers—their heads were big and swiggy, their grabbers out and their big carved teeth bared. They drooled and growled. On the other side, the snatchers, who looked out from the trees with empty teacup eyes, thirsty, then hid again. They snickered and lurked.

The chompers and the snatchers have reading and writing. I admit their poems are beautiful. Many concern our deliciousness, or the glory of the hunt.

In their forest, they menaced us on both sides, but they dared not cross the line, the line that our piss-yellow ribbon was meant to recall. Our eldest said the chompers and the snatchers used to be one species, in the days before language. They could smell the territory line. We could not, so the ribbon. The ribbon to mark their ancient division—a line of truce, of stalemate, of "cross here and all hell will break loose." They gave it a berth. That gave us a lane.

We were near the start of our two-day journey, of walking along the ribbon-line without cease. The forest was densely dragging itself down, vines and mosses dragging trees down into brush, the earth dragging down fallen logs. The chompers jeered at us. A snatcher threw a pulpy fruit and it glanced off the flank of Jut, but she did not stop walking.

Simon grew antsy, pawing and swiping on Ada's back, so I lifted him off and set him next to me to walk on his own. I pawed him some dried hay from my pack, still walking. We could not pause to rest.

A simple thing, maybe my fault, set everything off. Simon, who I had only just put down, matched eyes with a snatcher in the trees. Before I saw to stop him, he left the line and walked toward the snatcher.

I did not think then, I just went after. Still holding the ribbon, I bent the line. The others stumbled after me. One thing followed another, quick and without sense. A snatcher gave a mighty screech to alert its own others. Like a ripple through the piss-yellow line, members of my herd were tripping and falling and someone gave a mighty yell. There was a break—someone stepped too far off, and from where I stood, I could hear screaming and shouting and the soft clank of packs being dropped to the forest floor. It was a sickening feeling, the piss-yellow ribbon going from tight to slack in my paws.

When the ribbon went slack, many dropped to all fours and scattered. I didn't blame them. The ribbon bent to touch the ground, fluttering. We lost sight of the safe lane. All around were trees and pockets of darkness. Many screamed and yelled, but I learned a thing about myself, which is that I do not yell or scream.

I bent to pick up the line. When you spend your life as prey, some fantasies occur to you, often, of all the ways you might act if you were not prey. If you were not prey, you'd be the fiercest thing in the forest. If you were not prey, you'd run right at the things with big teeth, with claws, with sneaky eyes and ragged, thirsty mouths. So I held fast to the line when the others ran—I did not blame them—and I yanked the line out of the hands of those others who stood there dumbly holding a limp ribbon, a tradition already dead, and when I had gathered enough of the piss-yellow ribbon in my paws, I knelt, and when the inevitable chomper came rushing at me—like all his life he'd dreamed of this, of such easy hunting—I refused to be easy hunting, and I caught his rushing knees in the ribbon, and when he fell, I caught his throat in it, and I wrapped round and round, and I pulled the ribbon. Some of every kind stopped to watch my unexpected fight back, and Simon looked too, and I am glad he saw, as he scurried to a good hiding spot in the head-high grasses, saw the ancient line take on a new shape, saw me choke our age-old frights to death with it.

Reentry

THE IDEA OF moving her hands through clay enticed Frankie. It was a dark time in her life—she knew it even then, knew she would talk about it that way later, though she did not know when later would be. Her physical therapist had said she should occupy her time, volunteer maybe. Instead she signed up for a pottery class at the rec center near her parents' house. Signing up meant writing her name on a legal pad with a spotty ballpoint pen. So close she didn't need to drive.

The teacher was a white-haired and rosy-cheeked man, Greg—Santa Claus on keto. His quilted jacket was cut for a woman. By the end of the first class, Frankie would decide that he was pulling it off. Greg was a volunteer. The class fee just covered facilities and supplies. The other students were younger or older than Frankie by decades—school-children or retirees.

First, Frankie made an absentminded clay turtle that fit in her palm.

She thought she might give it to her father, to thank him for housing her, for not asking about the accident even as she took the stairs up to her old bedroom one at a time. The turtle was simple and clumsy, not a pot at all, but Greg came to the front of her worktable and bowed his head for permission to pick it up, like it was something sacred.

"Sure," Frankie said. She'd never done pottery before. Was this how artists behaved?

"What a precious little creature."

The turtle dried on the class shelf for a week, then when Frankie fired it in the kiln, its thumbprint turtle head cracked off. Elsa, one of the older students, found her first pot had exploded.

Greg called all the students over to the kiln. They stood in a circle around its squat cylinder form, looking down at its heavy round lid, its serious hinge.

Greg briefly explained techniques to prevent such catastrophe.

"It's natural, to be afraid of breakage," Greg said solemnly as they considered the kiln, "but you cannot. You try, try your best, to be sure a pot is sound, but eventually you've got to fire it. An unfired pot is not a pot at all."

Frankie looked around at the others. Were they hearing this shit? Elsa was nodding bravely. Frankie wasn't sure if she should giggle or write these words down. None of this, Frankie decided, was a big deal. Perhaps these people's lives, unlike hers, were very small. They knew nothing about fear.

Still, when it was time to fire a little green bowl, she hesitated. It was such a big kiln, such a hot fire, such a small bowl. When she finally lowered it into the belly of the kiln, she could feel Greg watching her from across the studio, approving.

• • •

Frankie sat down at the throwing wheel and winced, using her arms to hoist her leg into place. She had broken it in three places; the parachute had only softened some of the blow.

She steadied her foot against the pedal. Assuming this careful position brought to mind the moment just before ejecting from her cockpit, the electric importance of posture so as not to break one's spine, pulling in her limbs before the blast, slamming into the wall of air, the blackout.

She did not wet her hands before touching the clay; they were already sweating.

· · ·

At the beginning of every class, Greg passed around a cardboard box of fruit snacks. The students tore the packets open with still-clean hands and popped the gummies in their mouths. They were the good fruit snacks, translucent like colored jewels. Around week four of twelve, Frankie realized she had come to relish the moment of catching the serrated edge of the packet, finding give, the ceremony of the start.

Frankie started collecting images to show Greg later: the pucker of a strawberry, the contortions of a tossed pillow.

"Delightful!" he'd reply, before continuing his quiet rounds around the room.

She began noticing the place on every coffee mug where the handle meets the hollow body. Under the clean glaze, that clay must have been scratched and scored. She knew this was a permanent addition to her brain: her attention to that particular spot where constitution was uncertain, tested by firing.

· · ·

Soon, Frankie began to feel Greg's influence in other parts of her life, where he was not: a warm approval hovering over her shoulder as she selected her groceries, greeted her parents' neighbors, scrubbed the burnt bottom of a pan. All the things a person should be able to do.

The kiln continued to strengthen or occasionally mutilate their pieces. Some mugs lost handles; cracks creeped up vases.

Frankie had begun to think of her days as pots; shapeable, fireable—potentially even beautiful. She believed weeks and years might soon seem to be, too.

When the next season came around, she reenrolled in flight training, walked the halls of the base again.

• • •

Twenty-three years later, in orbit around Europa, Frankie listened as her commander explained the situation was dire.

The windows of their shuttle were small; Europa loomed blue brown, massive, scratched, and scored. Their journey of four years was compromised, the extent of the damage uncertain. They floated in a rough circle to discuss their options: attempt landing or abort. Any number of things might go wrong. Any one was enough. Comms to mission control took forty-five minutes one way. They had to decide. They all turned to glance at the hatch to the lander: its heavy round door, its serious hinge.

Frankie signaled to the commander that she had something to say. "It's natural to be afraid," she began.

A warning light blinked. In parallel, the team made their preparations: tightening Velcro against Velcro. One by one, they entered the belly of the lander. Frankie hoped that if Greg really were watching her maneuver in the zero-G, it would look as though she were lowering herself into the kiln.

En plein air

BEING A GHOST feels like nothing so much as a fever.

I can remember being laid low with yellow fever in the summer of 1911, taking little sips from a copper basin of cool water. I had asked the house girl to just stand there and fan me. Sometimes I talked to her like she was my mother, who had crossed two years prior.

Like my mother would, the girl scolded me for talking fancifully. They kept me isolated on the second floor of my sister's house in Atlanta; I could hear her and her husband and their children slamming doors below, but, for fear of catching my affliction, no one came to visit me except the girl.

I was confused, but not discontented, then. They say Géricault did his best work in the throes of a fever. I can believe that. I asked the girl to bring me my paints, but she would not.

They determined me delirious, but I had the sense I could see very clearly. I had forgotten I had fingers, but I found them. The edges of me felt untidy, like I was seeping right into the sweat-steeped sheets. I almost cried when the girl changed them, as it was like losing an intimate aspect of myself.

I got better. The fever quelled.

I lived another twenty-three years.

I died. Then the fever returned.

• • •

If you could see me, you might see my white dress and my green velvet sash, a curtain pull I repurposed: a calculated oddity that became my affectation. I could not paint without it. As when I was alive, I have no shoes, no brassiere, seeking to be free from constraint, to live more authentically and beautifully. But I am invisible.

I have haunted Ghassee Island for ninety years. More accurately, I haunt the visitors, who are blind to the majesty of the island.

My ghostly form seems to me to be the age I was when I lived at Ghassee for the summers: to myself I look twenty-seven. In life my hair was honey brown and sun warm. I let it grow down to my waist, beyond—I was quite proud of it. A hundred brushes in the morning and then again at night with the horsehair brush all the way from France.

I wait underneath the docks, the brown-dark water washing through my ankles, for the ferry to bump up against the planks above me. I pick some soggy sweetgrass and weave it into the golden braid that crowns my forehead. I have to redo this every day. It comes undone as night approaches, bedraggled as the day folds into night. It suits me to look like a sea witch.

Once I passed, I found myself back, transported to this place that made me, the artists' colony of Ghassee, a few dear square miles. There are almost no vermin, no mammals on this small barrier island. The territory is too small to support a coyote. Only I am predatory, endemic.

. . .

The ferry arrives.

Aboard are fifteen people, most of them familiar to me. This is the annual retreat of a small company, Ricochet. I don't concern myself overmuch with their occupations: I've long since stopped listening to their flaccid conversations. Though they have taught me many new terms, with their habit for combining meaningful words into ridiculous vacancies: *body consciousness, journey mapping, corporate giving.*

Conflict resolution. Cowards. If anything, in our reign here, we sought to stir up conflict, to find its tense center. When we were alive here—painters, sculptors, novelists, composers—we talked of the ideal ways for men and women to be together without restraint; of how to eliminate the scourge of poverty; of what the pagans had right and how to translate their raw genius to the needs of the new century; of how our works could be medicine for the masses.

What do these interlopers know of wearing morning glory crowns, passing a warm bottle of strawberry wine, growing crimson in the face? Of living unashamed, filling the long summer days with our best thinking, our bravest craft? Everything allowed us to focus on art: the dirty dishes spirited away, the studio cleaned, the bowls of paint replaced with new each morning, full and fresh.

. . .

As the retreaters disembark, I wrench the pier pilings. I am granted only minor interferences with the corporeal realm, so I must be precise. I could not make a soufflé, but I can swipe an untended egg off a counter. I am often mistaken for a sudden gust of the Atlantic wind. As with my paintbrush, when I yet lived, I combine little dabs and strokes to create an entire atmosphere of distaste and unease.

I cause the deck to shriek and shudder. An ominous warning. But Sylvia, my favorite prey, is the only one with sense to hear, to be shaken.

Sylvia thanks the ferry driver. Her round dark face reminds me of my girl, Josephine's; perhaps that is why I favor her. She also brings to mind the raccoons that populate Ghassee Island, my particular friends: scurriers, investigators. Round, dark, and disturbingly unbothered by either. She is last off the boat. She takes a deep breath and straightens her visor.

Now I reach up and brush the soft underside of a gull with a long bare fingertip. I give a sudden scratch; I incite it to swoop down at Sylvia, curved claws toward her braids.

"Ahh! Get away! Jesus!" Sylvia spills her iced coffee.

"Almost got you," a colleague tells her.

"Almost." Sylvia smiles uneasily. She is the only Black employee of Ricochet, though that's not a term I would have used when I was alive; it's one I learned from watching the company's equity and diversity circles.

What's this? Someone emerges from behind Sylvia, someone new. A girl takes a big running jump onto the dock and lands with a thump. She reaches for Sylvia's hand. This is the first year Sylvia has brought a child. Dark like Sylvia, hair in twists, knobby-kneed.

The girl lets go of Sylvia's hand and runs on ahead, toward the meadow, toward the barn, the big house with its hideaway bedrooms.

Though supposedly here for a retreat, the visitors seem not to grasp the concept. They bring the world with them, recreate its abuses in miniature, in diorama. They look at charts and believe that because they look at these charts in a barn by the sea, they will take on new meaning. They travel all the way out here and leave no time in their laminated agenda for roaming. They say things like "how refreshing" and "so good to get away," before locking themselves in their wired-up rooms in the big house.

· · ·

The retreaters reconvene at the barn. Though the silhouette is the same, it is not the barn I remember. The new owners have added insulation, blue carpet tiles, and hanging fluorescent lights. A bookshelf near the entrance holds yoga mats and pillows for those who partake.

I curl spiderlike against the ceiling, where once there was a heavy wrought iron chandelier and naked candles. For solstice, we'd hang bunches of dried lavender, and Anderson, the composer, would play the violin so fiercely the flames seemed to listen and dance along. Even the staff would come and listen, Black men hanging near the doorway with their caps in their hands.

To commemorate midsummer we'd crack our own stone crabs over a wicked fire and suck the juice out, plucking the meat and licking our fingers. We sought the simple righteousness of the sea turtle hatchlings, emerging from their mounds on a full moon and following that light to the Atlantic.

· · ·

The first night of the retreat I slip into bedrooms and pull on toes with my spindly fingers. Some startle and squint. But they soon retire again.

The next morning I trip the CEO right as he is about to begin a rousing anecdote. I hide the correct projector cord just before the whole-group presentation of annual milestones. I cowlick hair; I cause a cloud over the sun to block bare limbs from its grace. I team up with the undertow and make even the briefest swims fraught with danger, pulling seaward.

To survive, this place has adapted. The meadow has been edged and trimmed. The dunes are protected by a boardwalk, the planks of which are made of a material that will not warp or hold the warmth of the summer sun. There are courtesy spigots to rinse the sand off one's feet before returning to shoes and carpet. There are safety postings for the undertow, for the occasional sharks, for men o' war.

They mock our memories. I will rattle their windows open. I will let the insects in.

If I spook them enough, they will be startled into sight, might see me, might see Ghassee.

· · ·

When I was alive at Ghassee, I came back season after season. I am aware some said I overstayed my welcome. I was eager to produce work of merit. My medium was oil and my subject was the island itself: landscapes. In my hundreds of studies of Ghassee I strove to carve visionary truth, distinguished and unique. It was like trying to paint the wind by focusing on light and shadow, on the wind-bent grasses and the wind-gnarled trees.

Every morning my girl Josephine would pack up salted cucumber sandwiches and lemonade and follow me, carrying my paints and canvas out to the meadow or the shore. If I got in place early enough, the sky would still be purple gray. Too soon it would shift into lilac. Pale gold seemed to spend the day gathering at the top of reeds and trees and grasses. I could never keep up. The art of being *en plein air* is to forget the self and to be a spout for everything surrounding you.

I came maddeningly close. But my own slowness created moments of decision, and therefore corruption.

"That one's looking well," Josephine would say to an unfinished work.

"Do shut up," I'd tell her.

. . .

During a session on "identity and belonging," Sylvia becomes visibly uncomfortable. She starts tapping her plastic chair. Suddenly everyone is turning to her, deferring to her, performing their generosity on her. Artifice over art, again. When Elizabeth shares a story about her Black nephew, everyone's eyes flicker to Sylvia.

Sylvia looks up to the ceiling, right at me. I can't tell if she sees me. But this is why Sylvia is the best prey for haunting. She stares; she lingers back in team-building activities. She strikes off alone.

Sylvia has been my target for the last three summers. She grows in rotundity and wickedness every visit. She touches her forehead wistfully when she stumbles back to her room at night; she picks angrily at flecks of paint peeling off a bench; she shields her eyes to try to spot a trawler on the horizon. Of all of them she shows promise, seems capable of the skepticism and dread that makes tormenting her worth my while. She might be distracted long enough to see.

How do I haunt Sylvia?

I make the branches curl into and against the gutter outside her window and scrape moans in the wind. I lightly thump in the night, almost the sound of someone coming up the stairs, if you are already inclined to be superstitious. I tighten her shoelaces so she is slightly off-balance and achy all day. I entice the squirrels to dart in front of her at the last second—a startle. Sylvia reliably looks after them as they dash away. Such are our conversations.

At the shore Sylvia does not wade out farther than the rest—in fact, some of the competitive younger ones go out quite far—but sits herself down and immerses herself in the shallows and lets the waves tumble her around.

I want to hold Sylvia's head under water, till she comes up dead or refreshed. So, I do, for a moment, enough to terrify, my hand suddenly strong and firm on the back of her neck, pushing her face into the water and relishing her brief desperation for air. She comes up gasping and gulping. When she surfaces, she searches to and fro. She does not see, but Sylvia knows something is out there. Out to get her.

. . .

Clarice, the sculptor, once called my paintings "quite pretty." We were at dinner around the big table. I wanted to throw my plum pudding in her face and smear it all around with my coarsest brush. Everyone, it seemed, was enchanted by her at Ghassee. She sculpted women: muses and goddesses and furies. There was always some new Black laundress, commandeered from her daily duties to pose with just a sheet over her bottom half. These women provided the bodies, and Clarice had her special friends provide the faces. I was never invited to model.

Her work was deemed "significant." Still, they all looked the same to me.

She and Anderson started an affair and then lived together for another thirty-five years in Cincinnati. She and Anderson are just bones now, but I am still here at Ghassee. No one speaks their names anymore. I am the only one left and, it seems, the only mark. Our paper lanterns, our flower crowns replaced by plastic and Styrofoam and pleather and vinyl. I've looked for my old work, but that too is gone, my canvases, most of which I left unfinished, probably tossed out in one of the renovations.

. . .

I had not pictured Sylvia as a mother. I lean in from my ceiling corner to hear her daughter's name: Aubrey. I watch Aubrey. Aubrey is always running to and from her. She wears a too-large sweatshirt and cutoff jeans and many colorful barrettes to keep her twists in place. She is often barefoot, which I approve of. She is curious, turning away from the crowd and toward the trees and the shore, even more so than her mother.

I suppose Aubrey is here as Sylvia's guard. Sylvia was very badly behaved during last year's summer retreat. The man she slept with, Eric, is back as well, but this summer they are giving each other a wide berth.

Last summer when Sylvia and Eric slipped away into seeming solitude, I amplified their grunting and gasping, making it carry through the walls and on the warm wind, into every open window. Once Eric left and Sylvia was washing up, I showed her my reflection in her mirror, my judgmental glare, over her own similar expression. Just for a moment our eyes lined up, and she saw a truth she could interpret two ways: that she was being watched and that her own face was full of self-spite.

Really, I sought to jolt her awake. She was wasting that precious thing, her dissatisfaction, on that man, when she might have gone out roving. It could have been put to better use.

But the daughter is an interesting subject. Perhaps even more useful for my work. She comes up to Sylvia's waist, seems stretched out as if on a rack. I can't guess her age. I never had children of my own.

. . .

In the winters now there are no, or few, visitors. It gets very quiet. But still I am unable to paint. I lack the materials, nor might I maneuver a brush in any manner that satisfies.

So instead I explore new mediums: air, sand, branch, tide. I goad the ghost crabs out of their hidey-holes with the rank odor of a dead grouper, after high tide recedes and the sand is firm enough. I twist the scent upon the air to guide their paper-light steps. To me, what I direct the crabs to inscribe on the sand is a landscape—there is the meadow, there is the light infiltrating it, there are the dark sea-whipped trees. But I can hear the critics: there is no focal point, no tension, no revelation. My limbs are hot and I want to scar the earth.

If anyone were looking at the swarm of dragonflies, dancing and picking mates over the stiller shore of the channel, if they were to look in the negative space where the knowing insects refuse to wander, they might see the outline of a woman reaching out, orchestrating, trying to make a print of this place on the unfaithful, fickle sand.

Her hands droop. Her shoulders slump. She is unsatisfied with her efforts. It is still not right.

But now Aubrey is here and I will try anew.

. . .

There are no other children here for Aubrey to play with. She rejects the empty playground they built in our sacred meadow, glinting empty and hollow in the summer sun. She has become wild very quickly, abandoning her shoes and weaving bracelets from seagrass and half-moon blue-white seashells. She pokes stranded men o' war warily with thin reeds. Finally, someone familiar to the spirit of Ghassee as I knew it. I put my fevered hand on the back of the child's neck. But I do not shove or twist. Aubrey will be very helpful in my next piece. Through her I can do more: I can show the others, the fools, the land they tread on is not sterile or safe but holds surprises, something they have not been able to tame.

Aubrey follows the first risers over the dunes to the shore, where they lie down in their clothes on the sand, still wearing rubber shoes. They begin to do their exercises, frantically. They wriggle their torsos on the sand in perfect unison; they touch their elbows to their knees, and then their fingers to their toes, and on and on. They count like imbeciles, to twenty, incessantly, as if to evidence they know how. With their little thrusts and unseemly grunts, it looks like they are copulating wildly with the air. Aubrey giggles.

When the corporate crowd heads into the water, Aubrey and I look for strange tokens to leave in their pockets and their abandoned shoes. She picks up seaweed, wet, an owl pellet, a cattail, a miniscule dead crab.

· · ·

Aubrey doesn't need much prompting to go to the shore at night; it is an easy time to draw her away from Sylvia. I rouse her by disturbing a mockingbird into the old glass of her room's window. The bird, offended, darts away. Aubrey peels away from Sylvia in the bed they are sharing.

She sock-foots down the hallway, past the rooms of the business-people, down the porch stairs. The island must seem very safe to her. There are no fences or gates that signal she is not allowed. None of the regular rules need apply.

The big house is raised, so she descends and heads across the meadow and over the dunes and down again to the soft sand between tides.

Does she have the reverence for all of this—the meadow, the lapping water on the shore, the foam, the driftwood, the secret tracks of early morning that will soon be washed away—that it deserves? She sits in the soft sand and pulls her sweatshirt about her tighter, balls her fists up in the sleeves. It is not really cold; this gesture must be instinct. She is a child unused to the warmth of the night.

I begin to sketch in my mind, and Aubrey pokes at the sand with a stiff reed. I gently nudge and guide her hand; with the reed she imprints the gnarls of the wind-whipped trees. For a moment, everything is full of promise—I feel the strength in Aubrey's hand, the precision of her thumb and pointer, and the resistance where the reed meets pliable sand.

Then Aubrey begins to drag the reed across what she has done, marring it, bored and destructive.

I yank at her hair, and she tips backward and gets sand in her hair, along her mouth.

Still, a start. We will try again.

I perch in a tree draped in Spanish moss with my toes and fingers gripping like a sloth's. My limbs are unnaturally long, extra jointed. To get Aubrey's attention I nudge the playground swings; the chains groan. I waft breezes—damp cold smells, chittering sounds—to nudge her to one of my favorite secret places: to the family of racoons that has taken residence in a rotting gazebo. It is almost obscured by kudzu vines, but Aubrey finds it. She pushes her way inside. She stands in the middle, looking through the roof to the constellations. In her face I see it: Curiosity. Awe.

The racoons' yellow eyes are like more starlight in the forest. As Aubrey's eyes adjust to the dark, she sees them. They are moving about her. She should be scared, but she is not. My fever rises; this feels right, a right step in the work.

But: a scream, a familiar voice, the dull splintering of wet, rotten wood. Aubrey and I turn, seeing Sylvia, who is both here and halfway through the floor of the gazebo, having fallen, her adult weight too much for the old floorboards.

"Fuck me," Sylvia whispers. "What are you doing out here?" she says louder.

Aubrey is already crouching next to Sylvia, trying to help her up by the armpits. I have retreated back to my perch. We were getting somewhere.

The pair hobbles back to the big house. They find a first aid kit, and Sylvia directs Aubrey in wrapping gauze around and around her swollen purple ankle.

"I just don't know what you were thinking, out there alone."

"I wasn't alone."

"You better not mean those racoons."

"There was a white lady, a creepy white lady."

"Aub, that's not a nice thing to say."

"No, not one of the Ricochet people. I saw someone else."

"You're too old for that talk."

I am full of pride. She can see; I am getting closer.

· · ·

There was one particular pink I was almost able to capture in all the Lord's complexity: that of the inside of an empty conch shell. A pink you can almost see your face reflected back in.

I requested a titanium-white base, but the tint Josephine passed me was tinged with blue. And not just that but it was abominably thick, when my gentle work required a wash.

"I'll remake them," she offered, "and maybe a nice pale yellow, a butter."

I squinted at the grass tops, where a glow was gathering. "No, a canary."

Her walk back to the house was only hurried at first; I watched as once she reached the dunes she dawdled and looked up, considered the sky. The urgency, the import of my work was lost on her, but that was to be expected.

I tried Josephine's pink paint. It was passable.

When she got back, I scolded her properly, and she left to join the rest of the staff in preparing our supper. The light, again, had gone.

· · ·

It is Sunday night, the last of Ricochet's occupation of Ghassee. My last chance to work with, through Aubrey. The retreaters, Sylvia among them, are beginning to file into the barn for their boozy finale: the corporate closing ceremony. They wear blankets around their shoulders and trundle in, sock-footed. They carry in pillows and candles and flashlights. They wheel in a karaoke machine.

Aubrey is not invited to karaoke. After her dinner of make-your-own tacos—cold tortillas, cold shredded cheese—she is released to run wild. This is ideal for my purposes.

Together, we go poking around the big house, which has been left unattended. Aubrey tests doorknobs, exploring. She opens a white service door and fiddles with the machines stored there, pushes all the buttons on unplugged and outdated printers with dark cords coiled on top—no electricity in them.

The machines are left to stagnate here, easier to abandon than transport off the island. I do not like to consider them. I spur Aubrey on with a slam of a distant shutter elsewhere in the house.

Aubrey and I move in wonderful unison: her hands, my prompting. Many retreaters have left their doors unlocked. We move their belongings just slightly, enough to unsettle, to stir guilt. Condoms from the floor to the side table. We open a baggie of weed, dribble a little out. We balance a hairbrush by the handle. We laugh.

Music is starting to pump out of the barn. It disturbs the island air and Aubrey's focus on our work. Through a bedroom window I see her turn toward the barn, decide.

I am eager to get Aubrey out into the meadow or onto the beach to continue work on my landscapes. But I have no choice but to follow her as she pads toward the barn and its gross hubbub. She wants to listen in on her mother and the other retreaters. I try pinching her in the ribs, but she just waves her hands as if I were a mere mosquito.

Carefully Aubrey enters from the back, finds the ladder to the barn's attic. She drops the ladder and begins to climb.

It is very dark, barely enough moonlight to make out silhouettes and shades. I will spook her out of here soon enough.

Jarring discordant music and poor singing rises, muffled by the attic's floorboards. I look about for something to knock over that Aubrey will hear over the din. It has been years since I have been up here.

I see something in the attic, something that if I had a heart would cause it to quicken. Instead, what I feel is the fever in me beginning to pulse, rise. Canvases—a cluster of canvases. My canvases.

I become a gust, like sucking in a deep breath, one I have been holding for decades, that goes all the way into my fingers and toes, and *blow*. A canvas flops to the floor. Aubrey startles. She turns, more curious than coward.

She hoists a canvas into view. Yes, these are the very ones Josephine stretched for me. Even from the back I recognize them by their dimensions. This one, three feet by four, had been one of a series, a study of the way the morning sun hits the twisted pine trees. My paintings have been kept after all. Someone deemed them worthy of study. Aubrey will see their potential, see my project, its import. I can guide her.

Aubrey pulls out her phone, casts its glow over the front of the canvas. My work has been painted over. Thick strokes, garish color.

This is not my painting. It is full of people: hunched over in work and open to the sky and wading in the water. I never put people in my paintings.

There is no center. It is poorly composed. No focal point, except something hovering among all the little figures, invisible in their midst, in the negative space between them, like they are dancers at a great ball.

Someone has taken my discarded canvases, my false starts. Someone prolific: there are dozens of them. Was this painter mad? And who? I must have known them. Perhaps the novelist? It would make sense that he would hide them, as inelegant as they are.

I do not find this painting beautiful. But I do not look away. Neither does Aubrey.

She shines the light of her phone with one hand and uses the other to trace the lazy oval of the meadow with her pointer finger. The painting is unmistakably Ghassee, as if seen from above, floating from a great, inhuman distance: the Ghassee of my time, before the addition of the dock and the playground and the boardwalk. Under an odd pink sky there is the barn, there is the shore, there is the channel, there is the big house with its shutters. Crude thumbprint faces everywhere, most brown, some pink. One plays a violin—Anderson? I move closer.

There is a white dress with a green sash. The pink-faced woman wearing it has her hands thrown up in explication or frustration or exaltation—impossible to decipher. Behind her a brown-faced woman is carrying an easel, a basket of paints, a canvas. For my *en plein air* sessions. I remember well, the sun on my shoulders as Josephine followed behind me, spot to spot, never quite right, as I connived to establish the perfect vantage point that would reveal, via light and angle, an essential truth, Josephine—

Of course she had been taking my paints. There they are, just next to the canvases: the familiar jars and pigments, long dried out. After mixing them, she must have secreted, thieved them away.

Josephine! A painter! I chuckle, a bitter, rough sound. Aubrey stills.

And the deranged choice to paint us right in, to paint the island full of people, staff—and their mundane routines. Baking, ironing, carrying heavy loads. Ignoble. There's the big oak tree I struggled to paint, but here it is not an otherworldly mammoth mother but a source of shade for the Black women resting beneath it. And the pink of the sky: it is that pink I had Josephine mix and remix again and again, each attempt a failure, aiming for the perfect belly of a conch shell.

I hear scurrying. Aubrey is headed down the ladder. I am left alone with Josephine's ugly paintings.

My fever rises. Josephine's audacity: to steal my paints, my canvases, bought with my father's money.

Aubrey has fetched her mother, excited to show her the treasure in the attic. Sylvia, eager for an excuse to leave karaoke, is clunking up the ladder, slowly maneuvering her twisted ankle.

If I'd known, I'd have smacked Josephine's hands for stealing. If I'd known, I might have shown her proportion and shadow. If I'd known, I'd have her fired and sent away, far from Ghassee. If I'd known—

I decide to destroy them—the paintings, the attic—to ring the warning bell of dread to the long line of profaners and thieves. Josephine is long gone, but I will administer belated punishment.

Grotesque thumping and sexual yelps emerge from the karaoke below me.

I will burn down the barn. It has been wretched for some time now.

All I need is a bit of flame. I can make it grow. The candles. I need them to light a candle.

I turn the barn's generator off. One flick is enough, one nudge of a wire.

The karaoke machine dies. The fluorescent lights in the barn flicker and snuff. Groans of disappointment, and from Sylvia, plunged into darkness halfway up the ladder, a yell.

I make myself very large. Across all of Ghassee, I hold the sea grasses eerily still, a daguerreotype. Perhaps this is my great work, one of destruction rather than creation. All along.

Sylvia topples over the ladder and into the attic. I do not want her to die. Nor Aubrey. But if they are too stupid to get out of the barn in time, so be it. I want them to barely make it out, to be shaken, to never forget.

Out beyond the shore, a sympathetic squid infuses the water with sudden blooms of darkness. I foment fear. I wait. All I need is a little flicker of flame that I can encourage and grow, tip over onto the synthetic carpet tiles.

Yet, in the dark, after I have snuffed out the light and sound, no one makes a move for the candles. Instead, one voice—I recognize it as Dave, the accounts manager—sings out a cappella. It is not very beautiful or practiced. I don't know the song. But it is a song of yearning, of love, of loneliness—that I know.

More join in. A conclave of little voices fills the barn.

Aubrey and Sylvia are using their phones as lanterns to examine the paintings. They are humming the tune that comes up to them through the floorboards, just loud enough so that the other can hear.

I am transfixed. Does my plan fail? Or do I abandon it?

I have not heard singing in our barn for a hundred years, a hundred solitary turns of the seasons. When I was at Ghassee and alive, once we sung in the dark like that: I remember singing with Anderson and Clarice and the others here, in the same dark, my golden hair up in braids, and we were not comparing our successes, but, for once, we were really together, singing just for the temporary pleasure of it, being together after sundown and knowing it would not always be so, that soon we would be called away.

I pause my machinations, shrink down again to fit in the attic, with Josephine's paintings.

"Wow," Sylvia says. "Look at that." She points to the barn.

She is seeing the things I have been trying to show her: the people who lived and died and tried here, unheralded, in this slight span between the ocean and the land, their works, their tenuous attempts. They were here; we were here. Josephine was here, who I might have known but did not, beyond flashes of teeth, brown eyes; her yawning, giggling, pursing her lips, daydreaming.

Maybe I may know her now, a little. Her paintings insist upon it.

In Josephine's paintings the sky is the particular pink of the inside of a conch, shades merging and running into each other from all the little jars she mixed for me, repurposed. The pink that is blue and white at once, too, implausible but *right*, an effulgent pink.

Sylvia and Aubrey are chattering about Josephine's painting. They are planning to share their discovery, their great find.

In their last respite before this great unveiling, the figures in Josephine's painting look up from their miniature clotheslines, their books, and stretch their limbs, loosening like runners before a great race. The painted people are moving. Painted me, Painted Anne-Marie, goes on ranting and throwing her arms about. Painted Josephine glances out of the canvas toward me. She stares hard. Then, she looks away. She drops the canvases and picnic basket and begins roving. I am seeing things overlaid, people overlaid, generations overlaid, skies overlaid: the way I once scared Sylvia with my face over hers in the mirror. I am haunted by Josephine.

The painted skies—one by Josephine and one by me, now—are pink. She has taught me it can be done. I see the people in the barn-dark, us singing in the barn-dark, the corporate retreaters singing, so close they could hold each other's hands. Painted Clarice and Painted Anderson go walking through the meadow. Sylvia and Aubrey point their flashlights toward them. They freeze. "They're holding hands," Aubrey says to her mother. Sylvia reaches for Aubrey's hand in the dark. She kisses it. The skies are a pink you can see your own face in, the face of the sky, the pink gloss of a shell turning in on itself.

I have always wanted to paint a landscape that prompts a revolution in perception, in thought. I have never done it. But I see it can be done.

My fever and the clarity a fever brings are rising in twin unison. I want to put my cheeks on the pink curve of the conch shell to cool them, to cool my hot forehead, to rest. The hardness of the conch shell is so smooth it is like a bed. What lies in the center of the shell if not solace? I crawl into the shell of the sky, where it turns in on itself, and to make myself fit, I grow smaller and smaller till I am—

The Wedding Table

BEFORE OUR gathered families Elena and I took our seats across from one another at the wedding table. It was small and round, on the dais, with chairs for just us two, and laid with the finest china. Someone had put out all the sauces from the shared community stockpile: ponzu, Worcestershire, teriyaki; A.1. and ketchup; yellow mustard and Dijon. Each bottle was half-full, brought out for only the most special occasions—saved, savored, and passed down. I'd seen them before, for ceremonies, but I had never tasted them. I wanted to try them all.

Maybe that's what marriage would be like: trying all the special sauces, together. Induction into a mystery. The end of loneliness.

I smiled at Elena, willing her to be brave. Her simple brown hair was tied up in intricate ropes. She looked like herself under her serious costume and painted-on eyebrows and lips: the same girl I'd fed calves with and danced with and sat behind in machinery class. At the center of the table the grill glowed. "The embers of the heart," sang the priest. At his cue, I warmed my cleaver over the heat.

Elena lifted her slender left wrist to the red tablecloth. I squeezed her hand in mine to calm her nerves. I leaned forward to get more leverage. She closed her eyes and I brought my scorching cleaver down, fast, and clean as I could, for her sake. The coagulants and painkillers worked. Elena never cried out, just breathed in quickly through pursed lips. Our guests murmured with approval.

Flames rose as I used my silver tongs to place her severed hand on the grill. Soon, after consecrating our interdependence, I'd use a silver cocktail fork to wrangle out the succulent bits. The audience politely clapped. She'd done so well, after all her fretting. Very respectable. Her expression was almost euphoric; drugs and adrenaline, and not a little affection. She used her good hand to wipe her eyes.

My turn, my left wrist. I rolled up my sleeve.

Elena was turning her own cleaver over the fire, one-handed.

Unbidden, I imagined a clarinet—an instrument I'd never touched before—the warm barrel suspended between both hands, my fingers gracing the holes and silver keys, dancing over it. Maybe I could learn to play. Maybe I would be great at it.

Dear Elena brought her cleaver down. I pulled my wrist away, jostling the plates. The cleaver clanged against the table obscenely. A wine glass tipped over and shattered on the stone floor.

Such disappointment in Elena's eyes. She said nothing. She stared at me, waiting. Her right hand lingered on the cleaver's handle.

I had proved myself selfish, the greatest sin in such times of hardship. "Unity over independence," said the priest.

At his words, the quiet and stillness broke open. My parents and Elena's began to help each other out of their seats. They reached the wedding table. They moved beside me, to pin me with their four hands, against the high back of my heavy ceremonial chair.

Mouse Number Six

I ROLL MY shoulders and touch my toes, getting limber in preparation for my death.

When I die, I will bend my back and flop my arms, knock my knees and shiver my heels against the sticky floor so it can be seen from the back mezzanine. Let's be honest, *The Nutcracker* is a ballet for children, and children want to revel in my demise. It has to be so over the top it goes beyond scary and back to funny again.

I am double booked this year, my two biggest parts yet: Clara, for the even nights, and the Mouse King, for the odd. Clara is the résumé builder: a real pretty, face-y part, my blonde hair half-up, my face made rosy with blush. "I'm grateful for the opportunity," I say. These are our big moneymaking shows of the year. For two weeks in December we get a live orchestra and whole families in shiny shoes. Kids gawk at the big crystal chandelier in the lobby when it winks at them during intermission. After eleven years, finally there's a bigger-than-life poster of me as Clara in the red velvet lobby, cradling the Nutcracker doll to my chest.

But on show nights, honestly, I relish the role of the Mouse King more. Rambunctious rapscallion is more fun to play than Clara's little-girl innocence. I exaggerate every gesture. I vamp. From within my foam head and eye netting, the audience is a dark hearth, reduced to silence, or tittering, or cheers. I'll do anything to make them laugh. I'll scurry and tumble. I'll pounce. I'll lead my minions into the fray.

The mice are local second to fourth graders bussed here twice a week for cultural enrichment. The San Antonio Boys & Girls Club has partnered with our regional ballet company to deposit the kids here from four to eight, to "keep them off the streets." Boys & Girls provides the snacks, the transportation, and the additional supervision of Lara, the chaperone.

Most of the company feigns exasperation, but it's invigorating, how new all of this is to the mice: the velvet of the seats, the echo of the stage, the bright lights. With them, I'm elevated from a tired twentysomething into a wise ambassador.

Lara, the chaperone, is hushing Rudy and Q, who are hitting each other with their long tails and making lightsaber noises. Q slices his tail into Rudy's neck and Rudy clutches at his throat. He dies epically, just like I've taught them: a little gurgle, limp wrists and elbows, stumbling forward, lolling head. Lara grabs the boys by their mouse scruffs, then puts a heavy hand on each of their shoulders. We "teaching artists" are instructed not to touch the kids, but Lara always has a hand on them, tapping them on the thigh or grabbing their elbow to turn them around and direct their attention. Mostly she does the hand on the shoulder thing, like a safety belt. Like if she can just hold them in place for a moment, everything will gel: their young slippery selves will solidify into something more sturdy and prominent.

Onstage, the Stahlbaum children are unwrapping their elaborate, living presents. Ballerinas unfold out of boxes. Violins pace and swell in the background.

Offstage beside me, my mice are illuminated by the up-glow of their Nintendo Switches, perched on costume trunks and scrunching their painted-on eyebrows in concentration. I wish they'd watch the action onstage, enraptured. Still, playing Smash Bros. on silent is better than when, in dress rehearsals, they pushed one another onstage in the wrong scenes, their little half torsos momentarily sliced by the curtain and the sharp line of the house lights.

Andres, Mouse Number Six, hovers at the very edge of the wings, all of him twitchy with presence, wide with listening. He flickers his fingers like a phantom conductor. When tonight's Clara spins, he twists his shoulders in place so that his felt ears swirl about him. I know from earlier performances that Andres will stay in costume longer than the others, watching the rest of the ballet unfurl well after the other mice have begun to sprawl and eat the Goldfish packets and waxy red apples Lara hauls in.

We told the mice not to bother learning the choreography. Unlike the Stahlbaum children in their petticoats and the toy soldiers in their pantaloons, the mice did not have to audition. They are only here two days a week. As mice, they don't need to be practiced or precise. The more disorderly the better; it's what people expect to see in their mice, their villains. We just say, "Mimic the Mouse King, follow behind me, do as I do, slide when I slide, hop when I hop, stab when I stab." The audience finds their off-pace mimicry adorable. Children giggle; their parents guffaw.

I worry about the unspoken, unpleasant racial dynamic that emerges, with the mostly white Victorian children and my mostly Black and Latino mice, but my crew relishes their mousiness and prefers their gray face paint over the foppish wigs. The dance lead offered a few of the more coordinated mice the chance to switch teams. The boys laughed; they shook their heads; they looked at each other like *what fools*.

The rest of the leads and I are all white, except for Tony, this year's

Drosselmeier, and in later acts, the nameless and shirtless Arabian doll.
I don't imagine the ACLU is going to infiltrate us and come down hard
on our regional ballet for discriminatory casting. I think it's good that
we expose the kids to ballet, to the arts, any way we can. But it looks
bad; it hangs in the air. Every night the toy soldiers take arms against
us, my mice and me. Every night we lose.

There's a lot of time to watch Andres, to watch the other dancers, to
theorize. I mean, not a lot of time, a lot of *moments*. Short spans when
I am frozen in place backstage, already in costume but not yet in character, when I can't do anything else because I've got minutes or seconds
to entrance, so from the shadows I watch my shiny strong colleagues
onstage, and for a second I see it, the thing the audience sees, the thing
I think Andres sees too, the glamour, the cocoon of the theater, the
shield of it against all the daily bullshit, the enchantment of ill-fitting
costumes, of the garish lights and stage makeup. It is a miracle, this
thing that's brought us all together. The ballet is better than any of us,
with its powers of conjunction, of conjuration, of hypnotism. From all
this human mess, something grand and majestic.

Lara picks some fluff off of Q's ears. The kids do love Lara, I think.
When they rush offstage, they whisper to her, "Did you *see* that?" And
she looks each of them in their eyes and says gravely, "Yes, of course I
did, I was watching the whole time."

She tells us things about the kids, salacious things, like their lives
are her soap opera. She whispers, but the kids can obviously hear. They
are right there. "Of course Felix can't remember his cues, his brother
was just *deported*." Or, "You know, Leroy's mother is in prison, so he
gets distracted easily; just show him one more time." I do not ask. It
seems easier to let it lie. To let the mice abandon all that at the stage
door and embrace being fully mouse and nothing else, a mouse among
their own kind. That's what the ballet offers: the chance to sink into a
temporary selflessness.

Andres is running the edges of his costume—his ears, the hem of his
gray fur shirt—through his fingers. I get the sense he'd like to chew on

his tail but knows that would be childish. He keeps his costume tidy. No wrinkles; he must hang it when he gets home rather than dropkick it into a corner.

Even when I lead the mice in our most embarrassing warm-up exercise, the groin stretch, all spread and splayed barefoot on the glossy floor, Andres isn't one of the gigglers. "None of that," Lara tells the others. They wrap their hands around their little feet to force them together. Maybe I should do more to teach them discipline, but my time with them is so short. I try to be kingly, to mete out praise, all cold nods and "Nicely done, Simon." The mice are already in costume by the time I see them, and I'm not entirely sure how they get home after the show. I only know them for this odd interval between afternoon and midnight, rehearsal and performance, curtain up and curtain down. In the corner there is a pile of their abandoned sneakers: so many colors and sizes, some shiny and new, some dingy. I don't know which shoes go with which boy. To me they are all my mice.

Now Andres scrunches his pipe-cleaner whiskers and tries to plié, but his bare feet won't make a straight line and his torso wobbles uncertainly above.

He does a minor jeté and asks, "Like this?"

"Yes, very good." I nod. "Very mouse." His face splits into a grin.

Ninety seconds to entrance. Lara helps the mice line up behind me. I breathe in and make myself larger and more wicked. I can feel Andres's breath against my wrist, a half step behind me, first in line.

I've been thinking I should promote him to Mouse Number One, a purely ceremonial title. He tries to copy me so exactly, always at my right elbow. Each night when he leaves the stage, he is out of breath from high knees and scraping the air with his claws. Now that we have only four performances left, he anticipates my steps. He's memorized my patterns.

The other night he brought in a newspaper clipping from the *Express-News*, a pointillistic photo of the Nutcracker and me facing off in black and white. I wasn't sure what to do—sign it? I thanked him and tucked it into the mirror frame in my dressing room. Every night during makeup I consider its edges—perfectly straight but not scissored, just a little fuzzed: folded, licked, carefully torn, to preserve the fragile newsprint rectangle.

Onstage, the Christmas tree has grown to immense heights. The tinsel and lights rise and rise to the rafters.

It is our time—*entrance.*

I run flat out to center stage. I do a cartwheel and my mice tumble roughly behind me. I wave my scimitar high. I pace the stage like I saw a leopard do once at a zoo, deadly softness in the paws. The toy soldiers take a knee and fire at us but we twirl out of the way.

We are the sly piccolos; they are the righteous trumpets. They advance, we retreat.

After several volleys and early casualties on both sides, the music rises in volume, in pace, in shrillness. The Nutcracker and I circle the stage, circle each other together and tighter, looping into our inevitable final confrontation.

I prepare myself to get stabbed, to feel the whiz of the wooden sword past my armpit. I hold still, arms in front of my face in mock defense and cowardice.

My attacker never comes. I look to the Nutcracker, who is still several paces away, bent in half, reaching down, grabbing at something. It's Andres.

Andres has wrapped himself around tonight's Nutcracker, Brett, curling around his muscular calves, locking his ankles together. Brett tries to shake him off. But Andres holds on, flailing and flopping, as the Nutcracker stumbles and his great head wobbles. The other mice are already offstage; it's just the three of us now in the light. Only we can hear Andres say, "No, no, stop it." Andres's pink limp tail dances with each strain against him.

The orchestra is swelling, triumphant, signifying that the great battle has reached its apex and order has been restored. The familiar story goes on without us.

The audience is laughing. Andres—well-behaved, quiet Andres—has broken the ballet. We are off script, off book, off note, off tempo, off canon.

Brett has enough muscle to kick hard but must be thinking better of it. He gets one leg free and sweeps the other, dragging Andres on his mouse belly across the floor.

I am the Mouse King.

I cannot stand inert, my tail dragging on the floor. I start prancing to the rhythm of the notes to gain some time. I improvise a pirouette. I stand up straight. I salute Andres, my best mouse soldier—I'm not sure he sees, this is more for the audience—accepting his sacrifice, and dash offstage.

The audience cheers. A higher power—Julie, up in the wires—calls it and closes the curtain on the two of them, looming Nutcracker and little mouse, still grappling.

Brett escapes and rushes past me offstage to costume change. As he shoulders by, he yanks off his foam headpiece and gives me a quick shake of his red face, a *can you believe these kids*–type gesture.

Andres is alone for a moment on the stage, between the curtain and the scrim. He takes his time getting to his feet; he looks up to the ceiling, to the rigging concealed there.

Lara should go get Andres. I look behind me and she's busy barring our director from getting any closer to Andres, nodding ferociously. "Of course he won't be allowed to return. Of course I'll tell him. I'll talk to my boys. Yes, I know. It won't happen again." Andres lingers at the edge of the stage for a moment. Andres hears this; Andres is always listening.

He looks like a boy who is about to yell but he is quiet. I think he is trying to hide his crying by not crying at all. He must have practiced this before. Behind the scrim, stagehands are muttering and fussing. The ballet is still moving forward, like a leaky battleship.

Once Andres does cross back over, he is embraced by his mouse compatriots. They tell him it was "epic" and slap him on the back of his head. We are all stripping off our fantastic parts, unpinning tails and peeling off clawed gloves.

Andres turns his face into Lara's side. "I'm sorry," he tells her stomach, "I didn't—I just wanted us to win."

"Shush," Lara says. I can see Lara will defend Andres from anyone. From me if she has to. She does not have to. I try to tell her this with my face, but I realize I'm still wearing my mouse headgear. I take my head off.

Andres looks up to me and searches my face, that way children have of letting their hurt hinge on your reaction. We are all breathing hard. It is hot and tight and frantic and hushed back here.

I'm not good with words. That's why I dance. Andres's gaze is a greater spotlight than when I play Clara, alone onstage in just a thin nightgown. His eyes are watery and he is holding his hands in fists, waiting for a blow from someplace. It's clear I need to say something. Andres sacrificed himself to save me, to protect his kind. We all bend for the ballet—ask my hard pink feet, my tight waist, my practiced toothy smile—isn't that what we've been teaching them during these too-brief rehearsals? Submit, play the part, take the hit, join the chorus, die. But Andres believed in the ballet, the battle and his part in it, so much, so deeply, that he believed there might be a different ending.

I have to get into another character and be ready to dance the dance of the reed pipes.

I bow, low and theatrical. The gesture is not as noble as I'd like, given that a gaggle of sugar plum fairies bumps their way between us. My mouse head jostles. When I stand up straight and raise my gaze, Andres is already looking away from me, to where Lara is cradling a pair of off-brand, tidy small gray sneakers. She hands them to Andres. Really I don't know Andres very well, but even I can tell those shoes are all wrong. He never would have picked them himself. Now he is gray from head to toe. All the adults in his life, we have prepared this costume for him.

Tomorrow's performance will be back to normal. Mouse Number Six will be absent. The audience won't notice one less prance or high kick. I will be Clara—receiving bouquets, cheering on the Nutcracker; Andres will have to watch from the sidelines, if he shows up at all.

As Andres is being ushered away, the triumphant soap-flake snow is released from the plastic tarps against the ceiling. The Nutcracker has regained his composition. He is nobly landing all his jumps. Yet, from the darkness of the theater, I hear a murmur of laughter. Something is still off about the performance; something that can't be stilled and folded like Drosselmeier's human dolls. Something that can't be put back in its brocaded box.

There are one thousand four hundred sixty seats in this theater. One thousand four hundred sixty souls. They will remember; the children in the audience, those who are seeing this for the first time. They will think this is how the story goes: a valiant mouse soldier, a stumbling, fallible Nutcracker, and a Mouse King escaped, back to his mischief, licking his wounds and lurking along the edges, beaten perhaps but not defeated, living, learning to live, gathering strength and numbers in the wings.

The Man in the Banana Trees

I. TWELVE WEEKS

We lost the twins at the twelve-week appointment. The doctor was two hours late. Poor Dr. P., we were meeting her for the first time and she had to pretend for a moment that the ultrasound was ambiguous. We were all three looking at it: me, neck twisted awkwardly to look back over my shoulder, into the lo-fi screen, inside myself; Russ and she, staring head on. The absence of life was as evident as the life had been, the appointment before. The twins didn't have any names; we'd been warned not to do that so early. Still, we had a shared Google Doc going, just breaching into page 2.

The day of the D&C the weather was lyrically cooperative, from a story-structure standpoint. Just before I was knocked out, the rain started pelting, thunder echoing down the tiled halls of the surgery center. The nurses went to move their cars out of flood zones. They all had some glamour on for Mardi Gras around their scrubs and face masks: purple, green, and gold bandanas or fringe earrings, buttons or beads. The parades were canceled the rest of the week—they already had been for months because of the virus, but it was so cold that the city's collective bitterness dimmed and it all felt of a piece.

It would have been a rotten week for marching anyway. All the banana trees died in the freeze, or partially died, and had to be cut back to nubby, glistening bare stems. Brown, wilted strands faltered at the sidewalks.

The doctor was two hours late once more, so while waiting to be wheeled into surgery, I played word scramble games on my phone, gowned up like the circus tent of a house being fumigated.

My dogs believe that it is less intimate, less threatening to lick bloodied scabs off each other's eyeballs than to look each other right in the eyes. In the rolling hospital bed of the ambulatory surgery clinic, I felt very animal like that. It was daunting to look the nurses in the eyes while they hovered above me, saying, "Sorry for your loss," but easy to offer up my forearms for the IV, finger to the pulsometer, to scooch my butt around so they could access all of me more easily.

. . .

2. WHAT I SHOULD HAVE PAID MORE ATTENTION TO BEFORE

There had been a man in the banana trees—a regular illusion that never stops tricking me, the way the banana leaves flail like arms, waving to warn you. He couldn't have been taller than four feet, to retreat back into their fronds as quickly as I turned around.

. . .

3. UNSUBSCRIBE, PT. I

On the day we learned the twins were not alive, we were escorted out of the exam room into Dr. P.'s office, where we closed the door. I curled over my phone and began deleting and unsubscribing. The app where they tell you what size the baby is in fruit (two limes). The newsletter about reckoning with and preparing for a future taken over by twins. So facile—done and gone. I felt protective of my future self. Selected "no longer relevant to me."

The next few weeks the white dog would not leave my side. She followed me into the bathroom and rested her pit bull chin on my knee. She stood one cool paw on the flat of my bare foot. I tripped on her often. The brown dog was more reserved. This, his patient posture said, is not so unusual. He knows the stats. We are not so special.

· · ·

4. A FOUL NOTE IN THE TASTE OF GRIEF

It makes you self-centered. People were dying in Texas from the same freeze, but I interpreted every curling browned tropical leaf as a response to my presence, in accordance with me. If I'd lived in a medieval village, I might have been cast out: a woman who stillbore twins and brought on a hard freeze.

If someone said they needed to sacrifice my cursed body on the highest hill to make the weather better, I might protest, but I would think, *That sounds about right, that might work*. I would understand.

· · ·

5. THE WEATHER AGAIN

What was once tropical is wilting, bent underfoot, browning and bowed. What's that word for what they do to skin? *Flayed*.

Everywhere in place of the green and turgid there is limp pale straw.

The man in the banana trees must now be exposed—or has left for someplace else.

• • •

6. ON CRYING

There was crying, but that will be boring to keep repeating; the crying was boring and infuriating to live through, to keep crying and getting headaches and congealed noses and having to mouth breathe. So you'll have to just imagine it inscribed, overlaid over everything else: at first a lot of crying, and then less. You eventually run empty and have to eat or sleep or just take a break. You get bored and exhausted by your own grief. Here is a list of things that made us cry:

- Following the presurgery instructions: taking my wedding ring off, leaving it on the bedside table.
- Making grilled cheese.
- Making risotto (Russ), because he wanted to make more, increase the portions, feed a whole crowd, a full house.
- Russ's dream where they were born and were "really fucking mouthy." At first this made us laugh, but then we imagined the laughing we'd be missing out on. It was still funny, but we cried.
- Anyone being nice to us.
- The thought "this is really coming together" as I am writing this (heartless).
- Sitting on the floor strewn with cardboard boxes and packing foam, putting together a hall tree bought on Wayfair. I read the instructions wrong and drove a two-inch screw through a one-inch piece of wood and it burst out of the other end, punching through the veneer. Russ made fun of me—this was not the first time I had done something like this—but today our normal ribbing was too true: *I'm always*

fucking things up, I am overconfident, I don't double-check before reaching for the drill. Russ quickly said it was no big deal and we found the wood glue and he watched patiently as I glopped it over the ragged hole.

. . .

7. YOU'LL JUST HAVE TO TRUST THAT THEY WERE KIND

I don't want to tell you the things Russ and I said to each other. Or at least I will be choosy about it.

. . .

8. THE MAN IN THE BANANA TREES

The man in the banana trees is shorter than normal and he is physically disabled, the Dark Ages' signifier of wickedness. He is wicked smart; he will wickedly outplay you. He cashes in on how you underestimate him, belittle him, breeze right past him. His smile is twisted and lopsided. He stumble-walks, one foot larger and heavier than the other.

He was listening when you were foolish and flush with hope, perhaps laughing behind a hand to keep the sound from carrying.

He took our firstborn children, before they were named, and left me here with all this straw:

Baby books, pregnancy pillow that makes a cage around me as I sleep, ephemera, conversations with my boss about handing off my research projects, joy with no house, pills and needles and the red containers you collect spent needles in, well-wishes and excited texts, appointment reminders, unusable calendars, the month of July, the entire rest of time after that

We've been outplayed. I take to the spindle.

. . .

9. SIGHT UNSEEN

The first days after, I wanted to pay someone to sneak into our house, clear out all the uneaten food and replace it with new—full, fresh, and still in its packaging.

A friend had told me stories of how she was a Shabbos goy for an orthodox synagogue when she was in college. Easy money; the simple role of pushing elevator buttons and closing electric circuits for people who found the act unsacred. I could have used one of those, clearing the path for me, touching the hard to touch spots, darting ahead of me to sweep the way. To do all the daily tasks that suddenly felt inconceivable. I stashed the little onesies the fertility clinic had given us in the liquor cabinet to deal with later.

· · ·

10. BEFORE

He could have been under the floorboards, or in the ceiling, or even crouched behind the ultrasound machine on the day in January when we found out it was going to be twins. There aren't many places for imps to hide in the examination room, but he is immensely talented, and we were not looking. The doctor and I called Russ in from the parking lot to see, breaking the clinic's COVID protocols because it was such a sight. I think I swore, delighted. I was flush the rest of the day, with mystery and chance and the inexplicability of everything to come. Somehow it was less stressful, twins, easier to surrender—we would surely be overwhelmed by two, so had to go ahead and give up our urges to control everything. Russ grinned and grabbed my foot, which was still in the stirrups.

"What are twins?" I asked his brothers later—they are identical twins themselves.

"Best friends," Doug responded.

My grandma swore she had known it all along.

. . .

11. THE RIGHT NAMES FOR THINGS

On fertility message boards some women call this a "delivery," as in, "I delivered at twelve weeks." The medical test reports are indecisive, going with the euphemistic "product of conception," on one page, and the rather harsh "habitual aborter," on another. In text messages I avoid the word "miscarriage" because I never technically *had* one. The image it conjures in people's minds—of women bent over in pain, probably alone, in a bloody bathroom—did not actually happen to me. I don't want anyone to worry. I fall back on "lost."

. . .

12. KING CAKES

People dropped off cards, quarts of soup, flowers, and king cakes: kind friends. They snuck to our front door unseen, except one we caught descending our porch just as we were coming back from a dog walk. Russ and I were in pajamas, unbathed; we plastered on thin smiles and said, "Yes, we will call soon." The smile I gave was a grim grimace smile, corners tucked in, no teeth, polite and muted. It was the exact one from that "white people smiling" meme. That thought made me laugh, smile a real one.

The king cakes had little plastic babies in them, almost exactly the size, and my first thought was to pocket that detail away for writing this. *Will it read too dark?* I wondered. *Too on the nose?* Got to spin the straw into gold.

. . .

13. SIGHTINGS

Where had he been hiding? Every place we were joyful. In plain sight. He'd folded his small self into the footbeds of the backseat of our car, listening in as we called family on speakerphone: "No I feel fine, the tiredness makes more sense, high risk but normal."

In the very phone lines whipping in the wind, the waves of them. Him, pointy-shoed, the shoes we should have seen around corners but we did not catch.

Though he is lithe, the jingle bells on his shoes should have rung his presence. He is not subtle, but he goes after the blissful and blind. It is not because we cannot see him but because we cannot name him that we lose them.

· · ·

14. THE QUESTION OF THE REMAINS

I didn't think till afterward that maybe I should have asked for the remains. Is this a thing that more feeling, more spiritual people do? What are the protocols for that? Because I didn't even imagine this with enough time to spare; I didn't have the weight of choosing. I get to just wonder. I get to be stuck between, not knowing what kind of person I actually am. Forgetful, uncaring, maybe. The kind of person who doesn't even think to ask. The genetic testing fails, but I get a brutally biological summary of the biopsy: measured in inches, weight, color, and composition.

· · ·

15. HOW THE HOUSE SEEMS DIFFERENT (IN THE WEEKS AFTER)

The bedroom and shower become repurposed as places to go to cry: to meet the boat of feelings that waits on the horizon. To welcome the boat of sadness. We don't know what will disembark, but we go faithfully to meet it at the docks.

· · ·

16. NO BIG DEAL

If I don't get it down now, I might try to deny it later. *No big deal. We were wrecked, but now we are not.* I'd desperately like to skip to the end, sometimes, to *be* the wiser versions of us with this perspective, but I also feel a lot of tender love for the us still in the mire of it, still in the muck, wading out, clutching to each other each step. I know this would be a different story if I were writing it a room over from a baby just whinnying itself awake—but I only know this one.

• • •

17. THE BOOT

I start running again furiously, two days after the surgery. I have startlingly few symptoms; people online complain about far more. My tits hurt, that's it. I feel guiltily *less* impaired than when I was pregnant; I immediately have more energy and stamina and self-discipline. Just: there is a Band-Aid on my left thigh that I have no memory of receiving.

I run so hard after not running at all for three months that I rebreak a metatarsal I thought had healed in my right foot. I pull the medical boot down from a high closet shelf and, for a few days, I clunk up and down the front stairs and through the neighborhood, heavy-footed. I move slowly. The boot steadily reforms my foot when the foot lacks internal structure and fortitude. It makes my foot mimic and relearn the shape of a functional foot.

• • •

18. UNSUBSCRIBE, PT. II

Right when we think we've got that crying issue under control and are returning to some rhythms of previous life, someone who loves me texts me and tells me wisely that I don't have to be okay, that it is okay to feel what I'm feeling. To let myself.

I don't reply right away but I complain to Russ out loud: "But I'd really *rather* be okay. I don't *want* to feel what I'm feeling." I use a bratty voice; I know I am being fickle. He gets it, he nods. *I'd very much like to be excluded from this narrative.*

We make a lot of risotto. It's good because you have to keep stirring it. And because it is so fucking cold outside. Russ says he's glad we only gave fake names to the twins.

· · ·

19. THE SIDEWAYS SMILE

Another day in the afterward I go to the dentist for the first time in a year and a half. More straw: I'd made the appointment because I'd read that pregnant women should do this, that they are more susceptible to gum disease. I have two cavities; I have a mysterious piece of metal lodged in my gums. After the excavation and the filling, there is the familiar soreness and the way half my mouth lags behind the other, off-kilter. Water dribbles out when I sip. My smile, on Zoom, is lopsided.

· · ·

20. WHAT'S A GOON TO A GOBLIN?

—"mind so sharp I fuck around and cut my head off "—I prick my finger on the spinning wheel of my thoughts, the same device I'm leaning on to parcel out and spin up all this fucking straw; to spin it into this story, give it a glint, offer it up as something worthwhile: an artifact, a thing that is buriable because it is at least written down, more or less corporeal.

· · ·

21. ANOTHER FOUL NOTE IN THE
TASTE OF GRIEF

It makes you feel stupid for having been happy and hopeful, like you could have avoided it if you had been more careful, prudent, measured. *If we had been less confident, had less hubris, maybe we would have been less appealing targets for him.* I hate the thought that the happiness was an illusion, a trick we fell for. Russ insists it was not: that it was real, even if it is now gone. He saw it too.

. . .

22. THE BIG MEETING

I lay out the pieces of this narrative on a big empty conference table at my COVID-vacant coworking space. I move the pieces of straw around till—even if they don't make sense—they at least *resonate.* I relish looking at them. I lean back at the head of the table in my swivel chair like some kind of CEO, waiting to see what they have to tell me. I might accept their pitch, I might not.

. . .

23. ON THE EIGHTH NIGHT AFTER

We play hide-and-seek with the dogs, interrupting our normal paces to try to cheer everyone up. I hide as part of the coat rack. I turn into the wall so that no human parts of myself are showing, hiding my hands from their adept noses. I drape a coat over the back of my head and put a winter hat over that. It takes them two minutes to find me—a record. Russ hides in a dark bathroom, curled up in the tub. Even I can't see him, though I can guess where he might be.

. . .

24. BIRD'S-EYE VIEW

It is greedy of me, and perhaps unwise, to write this now, but I think if I wait I might lose track. It might be as if nothing ever happened at all. I can already feel it slipping away a bit; there are now days where I hardly think about it at all. I move through the house in old, reverted patterns; I diet; I lift weights; I shove stretchy pants into the back corners of drawers. If you could have a view from above, you'd think nothing had happened at all: a couple who makes dinner, eats it in front of the television with their phones out, sharing the things that make them laugh, leaning into each other. Maybe they sit a bit closer, maybe they are more forgiving about the phones and the need to go to bed early and lie sleepless in the dark for a little bit; maybe they are a bit more gentle with each other, asking each other how they feel with more regularity and really wondering at what the answer will be.

· · ·

25. LET ME TELL YOU A SILLY THING I IMAGINE

He must have thought he won the lottery, the man in the banana trees—such sweet targets, such marks, and two children to boot. Sharing in our delight. Maybe it is here I begin to empathize with him. Because to steal something, you have to treasure it, right? Maybe this is why I am so insistent on conjuring him up. He saw it too. He treasured what we treasured, saw value in what most people didn't even see at all; what they don't know is now gone.

I've decided I can't be mad at the man in the banana trees, the guardian of the children who were once ours. I think maybe he has retreated underground, his time here done. I hope it is warmer there. Perhaps he is raising them to be like him: to walk stealthily but assuredly and with secret names. We only get to guess at them.

Midnight Revolt at Bertrand's Year-Round Christmas Store

WHEN MAX WAS eight his favorite spectacle was the back wall at Bertrand's: a whole wall of snow globes. Each flashed a circumspect winter scene: no empty strip malls, no scorching parking lots, just snowy church weddings and sleds making their way downhill. Every forty minutes, on slower days, an employee dressed in red booty shorts and snowflake suspenders turned over a selection of the globes so that their flakes drifted downward, furiously slow, catching customers' eyes.

The store faced the Atlantic, across Florida's stretch of the A1A. Air-conditioned tours stopped on their journeys down to Key West to enjoy the novelty of candy canes in July. Max lived in a raised bungalow a block farther back from the sea.

Bertrand's kept the AC turned so high it was like entering another world. Older boys came to gawk at the hard nipples; Max came to breathe in the cold.

When Max was nine, his dad stopped calling. His mom finally caved and let Max pick out a snow globe of his own. Max had had his eye on his special globe for years. On tiptoes he reached for it, top shelf, fourth from the left: a city ice rink, a skater in a short purple dress arching her ankle over her high ponytail. Behind her, every skyscraper window was alight. Max imagined his own skirts, swirling in the cold, him the one carving fiercely into the ice with very sharp shoes, knowing that one particular yellow window in the tall, anonymous city was his entirely.

Max shook the globe. His mother frowned. He swore the tiny skater was gliding. He did a twirl. His mother pulled his hand to still him.

Max grew his hair long, in a high ponytail just like the skater's, a solitary, defiant *swish, swish*. He peered into the snow globe, tracing the intricate patterns she carved.

At thirteen Max picked the globe up out of its lacquered stand. It was heavier than he remembered. Some boys in school had taken scissors to his ponytail, *snip, snip*. They had spotted him, spotted her, the part he'd shrunk so small and closed up in a globe and left on a shelf. He lay back on his bed and placed the globe on his breastbone so that the little enclosed woman would skate into him: *slice, slice*.

The skater landed on one foot, with a flourish of her arms. Max wanted to hate the skater. Tomorrow he would get rid of the globe. He would ask his mother to buzz his hair down to the scalp. But for one more night he wanted to feel the weight of her, her city, its different sky.

Max awoke to a dark room. The globe was swaying, rocking in the center of him. He could not catch it in time. It rolled off him, onto the floor, cracking and spilling there on the laminate boards. Minute snowflakes salted the floor.

Max offered a finger to help the skater up from the shards. She spoke; it was like the flapping of a hummingbird's wings, unintelligible and insistent. Max wanted to understand.

She squatted and then jumped, leapt against Max's window like her legs had grasshopper springs, like she was trying to tip over the whole house like she had tipped her globe. *She must be trying to get home, get back to her own kind.* That was what Max would have wanted. She fell back on the floors and started skating angry figure eights. Max's mom would be furious about the scratches.

The skater needed him. He could bring her home, to Bertrand's. Max found a Dixie cup in the kitchen, put an ice cube in it, set her in it gently like he might a pill bug pet.

At Bertrand's, the skater got agitated. Max could feel her banging against the soft sides of the cup. He heaved a concrete Nutcracker through the locked glass double doors. Alarms blared, setting off a cascade of Santa's jingle bells rocking.

At the back wall, before he could place her on her high shelf, the skater began her call. Amplified by the mouth of the cup, it sounded like a dryer spinning so fast it might take off.

Her kind heard and understood. They rushed up. Shepherds and townsfolk and penguins and cobblers leaned into their curvatures, pushing and climbing. Their globes trembled, then fell into the plush red carpet.

They began to roll, a fleet of them glancing off each other, down the linoleum aisles and out, a clunky bulbous parade through the door, across the parking lot, then the highway, then the shore. The globes made tracks in the still-warm sand, crisscrossing and braiding into each other on their way toward the sea.

Max followed. He sat in the sand and took off his shoes. The skater was climbing at the lip of her cup to get a better look, so Max turned it sideways, away from the town and its light pollution, toward the dark sea.

Together Max and his little woman watched the globes enter the surf, bobbing, risking together the roughness of the open water. Max envied them their true north, their gulfstream current, their thick glass. They hung a left, toward the snow that is not bone or porcelain or soap flakes. They could not have made this trip before, but they seemed to know where they were going.

In the cup, the skater was still. She, globeless, was stuck with him. Her skates were part of her feet; her ice cube had melted. Max would find a way to keep her happy, keep her safe, keep her cold till they could go north together.

She opened her red bow mouth and spoke—the dulcet sound of ripe magnolias slapping into each other in a breeze. Max didn't speak her strange language, but she could teach him, he could learn.

In the Style of Miriam Ackerman

I EXIT MY RIDESHARE and find the pamphlet from Aunt Mi's funeral in my jacket pocket. That must be the last time I wore this suit, my only suit—three years ago. *Funny*: one last joke between us.

The Rowe Art Institute's facade sports two dark banners announcing "Miriam Ackerman's (After)prints: The Digital Second Life of an Outsider Photographer" in stark white text, parallel to the fluted columns. The beaux arts building is beautiful, lit up in the twilight, boasting the name of the robber baron whose home it used to be. So many bedrooms, now turned into galleries.

Arrived, I message CarelessWishbone91. Instantly I get three emojis back—all hands—which I've learned they prefer to words: 👋 🙏 👍

Maybe the emojis are less incriminating if we ever go to court.

Someone hands me a guide to Miriam's exhibition. I tuck it, along with my warm phone, into my pocket. It kisses the pamphlet from her funeral.

As Miriam's nephew, and one of her only living relatives, I've been invited as a guest of honor. I was the one who found her negatives: after the funeral I stayed extra days to clean out the empty bungalow in Biloxi. Aunt Mi had lived there alone for years. I had moved out after college, and mom had gone off to the nursing home. She should have just sold.

But instead she filled that house. I found negatives in the garage, the bookcases, the cabinets. She'd stored them in boxes, binders, grocery bags, and, in one case, a Dutch oven.

· · ·

Waiters swarm like wasps. One catches me and offers, from a legitimate silver platter, a small piece of toast. The toast is covered in a dollop of green, then cold cream, then a quivering scallop. I take one and throw it back like a shot. It is a curious mixture of crunchy and soft, salty and green. Aunt Mi would have scrunched her nose at it. But maybe she would have liked it, once she tried it, being a curious mixture herself.

Since her photos went viral, I've been asked over and over to describe her reclusive tendencies and eccentricities; for podcasts, for local news segments, for *Garden and Gun*, *Aperture*, and the *Oxford American*. They all expect me to act shocked that she had real talent. "Did you know? Did you suspect?"

Of course I did. I'm the little boy in the photos.

I was there when she lay on the cold linoleum floor of the Piggly Wiggly to snap a series of photos of me, age seven, from below as I considered a captive lobster. She'd wiggle one inch to the left, mussing her skirt, and snap rapid fire again. She'd angle the camera, craning her neck. Other shoppers would steer their carts around her and look back over their shoulders from a politer distance. Still on the floor, still swiveling to get the frame right. All that to get one shot, one right image. I remember the clicking. I remember wishing she would hurry up. In the resulting photo, it looks like I am trapped in the tank with the spiny creature as my companion.

Aunt Mi lived in Biloxi for as long as I can remember. She had her own bedroom in our house, was my babysitter, but we didn't call her that because she was my aunt. "Unemployed" was what my mother said. "A leech, a mooch." She drove me around for hours, crossing the railroad tracks, taking back roads. "Errands," she said, even if we just did circles: on I-10, then off again. She'd pull over if she saw something on the side of the road. I'd go on ahead and poke around and she'd take photos of me looking: at a road-killed deer, the haunch torn off; or at a tractor overcome by kudzu and jasmine.

I'm the boy in the photos, but no one seems to recognize me as I scoot into the gallery. Of course they don't. I'm in my forties now and all these well-dressed professionals look like kids to me. I might be the oldest person here.

I stick to the edges. I pass clumps of people in short sequined dresses, dangly earrings, smart jackets. Somewhere in the crowd, no doubt receiving congratulatory handshakes, are the museum director and the exhibition curator. I wasn't included on whatever Zoom call they used to set this all up.

Cocktails, food, and conversation dominate the main hall, but to actually see Aunt Mi's work you have to enter small dark rooms, sectioned off through mazelike entrances. Each photo takes up one whole room, surrounding the viewers. This "afterlife" part of the exhibit, I'm informed by the brochure, is achieved with two technologies. Projection mapping throws the image across all four walls, the ceiling, and the floor—immersing you in the world of the photo, like a silent observer, like a ghost. And, of course, since Aunt Mi's photos only existed in a limited frame of two dimensions, a sophisticated AI extends the images, generates new, aligned material, so seamlessly you can't tell where the original photo ends and the remix begins. "Almost as if," the introductory text proclaims, "new life is being breathed into these images of 1980s' small-town southern life."

Most people are going through the exhibition in chronological order, watching the boy in the photos grow older. But the lines are shorter farther back in the hall, and I figure I know the end; there's nothing to spoil. *I am the end*, I think. The thought amuses me. The hallway is a timeline of my childhood in Biloxi. I wonder if these people would be disappointed if they knew. I decide to begin in the last room.

A couple nearly bumps into me, exiting as I enter, holding each other by the elbows. "Provocative," one says. "Mm-hmm," says the other, "the consideration of form is reminiscent of—"

For a moment the hidden projectors catch my eye with a blinding glance of light, prismatic and direct, like stepping through a beam of sunshine in a dark garage. I hear them humming. Somehow this room, even its corners, overflows with warmth and color. Obviously it is not real. But it is easy to put on this reality.

What I see first is me. Not as I am, but as I was. *Skinny* is the first thing I notice. Fragile. I could pick up that boy and throw him. In the picture, the boy-me is floating face up, surrounded by dark water: the pool at our complex, at night. The lamps in the background are blurred to halos. The water, though, is focused and sharp, looks almost cutting. You can see the goosebumps on the boy's skin. The boy is frowning, and his thin arms are thrown out to keep him afloat. Almost Christlike, which is a weird thing to think about myself. He, I, must have been about fourteen. Though I can still hear the cocktail party and enthusiastic chatter around me, I have entered a different world, for a moment. My brain accepts the illusion, sinks into it.

I remember being embarrassed when she took this one. My body, on display, a subject, even if she didn't plan to do anything with the pictures. I was exhausted by the floating, and cold. I'd rather have been with my friends. But instead I treaded water, tried out different poses, waited for her to release me, to have captured whatever it was she was looking for.

The boy in front of me is searching the dark sky. Because the sky was outside the frame of the original photo, the algorithm has stitched together a plausible, likely sky, based on the play of light in the original photograph. Thin, high clouds, a brilliant half-moon. Look, they put a plane up there. I suppose it is statistically likely there was a plane above me that night. Its wings artfully reflect the spread of the teenaged boy against the dark water. I try to remember if there really was a plane there but I cannot. Can you remember the sky from a day thirty years ago? This sky, this childhood isn't mine. Whose is it, now? How dare they add a sky, a plane, these clouds to Aunt Mi's photograph? To my memory?

I am angry. I am fascinated. I look to the face of the floating boy and recognize the same expression in his face: anger at his circumstances, his body, the cold water, his aunt. But something in the sky has caught his eye, and despite himself, despite his best efforts to be brooding, he is caught looking, caught in wonder, by what he sees in the sky. He's hungry, but hopeful. Maybe life won't always be this way, this mundane, this closed in. He can see beyond it. You're made to root for him.

I turn to look where Aunt Mi should be, the photographer's vantage point at the edge of the pool. She should be there, crouching against the wet pavement to get low and create the expansiveness of the sky. But, the AI has stitched in a waterslide instead, one that was never there before. She's been skipped over, erased. Of course, she was so implausible, so one of a kind, so herself. That's what made her so intoxicating, and so frustrating: her unpredictability, her unwillingness to budge or to compromise or to explain herself. A waterslide is in every way a more plausible part of the picture than Aunt Mi.

· · ·

She was a heavy woman in many ways, not obese but inelegant, cloddish, always wearing a men's blazer—or maybe it was a little boy's, so tight on her shoulders it could never close—over a black turtleneck and stockings, so she was always flushed. Now that she's famous, people are labeling her as a lesbian, butch: easy terms to write away the things that stalked her all her life. "A kook," my mother called her. I'm sure some scholar is now writing a thesis on this very topic. "The Sexuality of Miriam Ackerman." Poring over her photos and her letters like they are clues.

I flinch; this is all my doing. I put her photos online. Most of them were of me, or I was in them, even if it was a picture of something else. I picked a few negatives and brought them to Walgreens. I posted my favorites to my socials. When people started commenting from Finland and Hong Kong, I knew something bigger than me had been let loose. Someone commented from Brazil, in Portuguese. I instantly translated it: "The look in that boy's eyes. Haunting." That boy was me.

I sold the rights to the photos. The pictures had taken off, and the lawyers I found said there could be serious money. The kind of money that would let me pay off the house, Angie's degree—the kind of money that I never had growing up, the kind of money that would let me travel to somewhere unreasonable. *The northern lights*, I thought. *I'd like to see the northern lights.*

I worried someone would use them in commercials. But the lawyers laughed that off. Imagine someone trying to sell deodorant or a Mercedes with an image of me screaming at a seagull that is flying off with a pitiful mylar balloon of a circus elephant. I put the photos up for auction. "You'll make more that way," the lawyers said. "A feeding frenzy; make the most of the momentum, of the moment." "Surely she'd want them to be *seen*," the appraiser said. "So many negatives. Or else why take them?"

But I knew even before then, knew her work was good.

Her makeshift darkroom was the bathroom between our two bedrooms, hers and mine, that we were meant to share. It was stocked with trays and chemicals she pilfered from the local community college. We developed a secret knock. Wait for the return knock, then you know it's safe to come in. I'd turn off the lights in my own room before entering; I'd pee surrounded by that vinegar smell and spools of film so often, it seemed normal. So many negatives, hanging like vine tendrils off the shower rail, obscuring the mirror. She developed all the negatives, cut her favorites out with scissors, but never made prints, never tried to sell them, never submitted them to anything or anyone for approval.

· · ·

A polite chime sounds: it is time to move on to the next room. The lines to enter the photo rooms are lengthening. A man pauses to crouch for a selfie with the floating teenager in the photo; making like he is splashing him. Someone else guffaws drunkenly. I say goodbye to myself.

I enter more pictures and encounter myself at ages twelve, eleven, nine.

There's one of me at my bar mitzvah, frowning in concentration at the Torah. The boy glances nervously out at the audience. The room he is looking out into is far bigger than our actual synagogue—Beth El in Biloxi had just a series of chairs in a room like a rec center, but this is some grand pewed synagogue with a high roof. "A bar mitzvah in the style of Miriam Ackerman," but not my own, not the one I actually lived through. The crowd is full of unfamiliar faces, not my family or friends or neighbors. Plausible, believable, but utter strangers. Maybe they aren't real people at all, but composites.

The thing that made Aunt Mi's work special, made people comment from Lagos and Amsterdam and Madison, Wisconsin, was that she was unpredictable, in her frames, in her angles, in what she centered. Here nothing is centered. The AI is trying to learn her style, to reduce her to something that is predictable. Predict, and steal. Stab, and twist.

I stand there trying to remember what she was really like. I remember she sped through yellow lights, like all of us, I guess, only she made a big deal of it, leaning forward and reaching for my hand like she was taking a great risk, like maybe we'd die right then and she wanted to be holding my hand.

I feel a buzz. CarelessWishbone91: 🌀

Not yet, I send back. I want to see a little more.

• • •

I know this photo. It's a controversial one. Aunt Mi was always photographing me at my most vulnerable. The cold pool, an injury, a tantrum. I'd stub my toe against a curb—*snap, snap, snap*—hot nights in the Biloxi house when the AC broke down and we'd all lounge around, them in slips and me in briefs—*snap, snap*. I crashed my bike into a parked van while learning to ride, and before tending to my scrapes, Aunt Mi photographed me looking down at the crack in my new helmet with wet eyes.

This one is from after Hurricane Elena in '85. The dumpster had sat at the end of our block for weeks, as people carried soggy trash to it. Aunt Mi photographed me playing in the bottom of that dumpster, sunlight pooling in from high above.

The boy, who is at our eye level, seems surrounded, wistful. He sifts through the sharp wreckage of the storm: broken windows and their frames, bent-sharp blinds, a blue tarp, shingles. The curators and their AI have extended the walls of the dumpster to wrap around all four walls of the room, generating likely trash to surround the viewers and the boy: there, a fridge, on its side, and—a sled? In Biloxi.

The boy looks so alone. You want to hug him, you want to protect him; or at least I do.

• • •

I skip ahead to the first room, the youngest iteration of me. As my eyes adjust to the dark I see a high chair in the tight Biloxi kitchen. SpaghettiOs are dribbling down the boy's chin while he turns around to try to watch a TV show behind him. A curl of smoke from his mother's cigarette drifts up toward the single overhead kitchen table light. The smoke makes an eerie approximation of his toddler shape, his gesture, so it looks like there are two of them there, keeping each other company. I start to pivot, to see the rest of the image that has been stitched together. They got the sink right: it's full of dishes. The curtains are drawn, yes, but they are the wrong pattern, some other 1970s' fabric.

In the original photo, my mother is cut off; just her wrist appears holding the lit cigarette. That framing, excluding her, seemed to me to be commentary on Aunt Mi's part. No one else can be in on her little joke because the jokes are gone, scrubbed away.

In this version, my mother is reinvented. The face the algorithm has given her is not her face, it's a magazine-mother face, an amalgamation sourced from advertisements. My real mother is in assisted living in Bay St. Louis and this one does not look anything like her. Here, her hair looks like it is collaged-in from a shampoo commercial, bouncy and shiny. Her face is full of attentiveness and enthusiasm I don't recognize.

There are no answers in that false face. I'm done looking for them.

I reach into my pocket and message *All yours* to CarelessWishbone91, who, unlike everyone else at this exhibit, is not a stranger, though I've never seen their face. Back in July, when I'd asked the message boards what could be done to take the photos back, to throw a wrench in the exhibit, CarelessWishbone91 had appeared as a 🖐 and sent me a link to a more secure channel.

Now they message: 🖐👌

I take that to mean they have set it loose.

The first sign of change I notice is in the voices of the gallery goers. Surprise and amusement: "Hey, look!" Throughout the tucked-away rooms, the boy in the photographs is changing. The audience sees familiar faces, perhaps their own, cast into the photos.

"That's so cool," someone says.

"Did you know this would happen?"

"How is it doing that?"

A nervous giggle.

CarelessWishbone91 and I have unleashed a new algorithm. It mines the pockets and purses of the audience—no longer just audience; now, subject. It is sifting through their files, their photos, and the displayed images—already collages—start to morph and twist further.

I'm still standing in the kitchen, which now shudders with rapid changes. The twist of smoke becomes a ribbon becomes a flame becomes a curled lock of hair. The gesture of the mother's hand changes, from holding a cigarette to an open palm to a manicured claw to a fist. Then a caress. So many pictures of hands in this room for the algorithm to process and weave. Each iteration only flashes for a moment before it becomes fodder for the next run-through. I don't know where it will end. Will it all blur together into mud? Will it ever be satisfied?

I don't linger long. I step out of the dark cluttered kitchen of my not-mother.

I want to see this unfold. I want to watch them catch on. I hurry back through the rooms.

The waters of the dark pool are merging with images of oceans and ponds and rivers. The floating boy goes from Christlike to actual crucifix. The crinkled crests of the water become wrinkled sheets. The bare chest of the central figure is replaced by nudes, nudes pulled from the audience's phones, morphing and merging, cobbled together but still recognizable.

"What the fuck?" someone hisses, close by.

In the bar mitzvah photo, the Hebrew on the Torah becomes receipts, contracts, screenshots of text messages, any words the algorithm can find, grasping for semblance without meaning. The crowd in the synagogue is dancing with the faces of the gallery goers and their loved ones, their pets even—I notice a Pomeranian in a suit. Any places the original photo showed exposed skin are beginning to be speckled by ingrown hairs, nipples, bruises, odd growths, and bug bites—all the embarrassing bodily phenomena we document daily.

The pictures are moving; they are moving because they are changing, linking like to like and jumping lily pad to lily pad between related forms, becoming new at every raw edge.

Someone yells. The audience doesn't like seeing what was theirs and theirs alone being on display or, worse, being twisted and combined with other lives: a familiar head grafted onto an unfamiliar body.

As I walk through the gallery, people are moving quickly, no longer at cocktail pace, dashing from room to room to figure out what is happening, to find someone to complain to, to demand they fix it. The exhibit is going to shit around me. Let off the leash, the AI is biting the hands of its supposed masters; the AI is just hunger, undiscriminating. I take another canapé from the platter of a confused waiter. I duck into the next room: back into the dumpster.

The high walls flicker: into a cathedral, into a slick cave, into a cenote, the light like we are at the bottom of a great barrel. A well. The boy is shifting: into other children, older, younger, faces covered in banana mush, eyes wide, mouth smiling, hands reaching. Maybe our new algorithm has set the boy free. The curators have the rights to the pictures. But I held on to the originals—thousands of them.

I turn and stroll toward the spot where I remember Aunt Mi was standing with her camera. From here I could reach out and hug the boy.

I remember Aunt Mi grabbed my hand and we climbed out of the dumpster together. We went out after for cheeseburgers, the chargrilled ones, at the stand that was my favorite, and she dipped her French fries in a mint milkshake and I told her she was crazy. She dangled a green-tipped fry in my face, and we laughed.

The boy wasn't alone at all. He was with the person who saw him the most, who relished the wildness in him, who gave him a few moments to breathe, to wonder at the dark and the light, before helping him out of the hole.

I look to the spot where Aunt Mi should be, remembering the flicker of her grin as she lowered her camera, the gesture that meant she thought she'd gotten it. Captured it, the something wild. The algorithm runs through a thousand sensible guesses for what to put in that spot next to me, the one she stood in. None of them are right.

The Pantheon of Flavors

KEYNOTE TALK (excerpt)
Mildred Moore, Independent Flavorist and Trend Forecaster
International Ice Cream Technology Conference 2036:
Beyond the Big Chill

Welcome. I'd like to talk about change: how our industry can adapt.

To begin, I ask you to imagine. Imagine you are walking into a classic ice cream shop on a hot day—and aren't they all hot days?—with its pale pink walls and the great counter-height freezer and the intoxicating smell of waffle cones, sweet and yeasty. You look up at the chalk list. What do you expect to see?

For my husband it is cookies 'n cream. For me, salted caramel. I will be saddened, confused, and disappointed if salted caramel is not there. These go-tos are what I call the "pantheon," the big gods of ice cream. We know they will be there, we seek them out.

These are the big sellers, the profit makers. There's not room on that chalkboard for everybody. The pantheon is an exclusive group. And, like the ancient Greek deities, they reflect the particular societies of their human subjects.

Let me give you a little example. In old doomed Louisiana, before the consolidation, children there grew up familiar with the flavor called "tiger's blood" for their snoballs. You could call that flavor a local deity, a minor god. The name and the red were so vicious; the bright red juice sliding down your hand caused you to imagine the tiger that was maimed and drained for your pleasure. How fun it was to eat the most majestic beast. To be decadent and evil, to demand such sacrifice on a hot summer's day. Then you see a tiger at the zoo, and you know it, too, is full of cold and sweet nectar. This flavor, then, acting as a reflection of children's bent toward brutality.

And in the Midwest, they worship at the altar of the moon: blue moon, a secret recipe. Some claim it involves castoreum, an exudate beavers use to mark their territory. Notes of citrus and vanilla. Regardless, the name, vibrant color, and mystery suggest to me a particular regional desire for the unusual, the elusive. Just as most UFO sightings come from that region, the land of crop circles—people desperate for a moment of something from beyond, something more than the familiar flat plains of landlocked sameness.

My expertise is in turning these buried collective compulsions into flavors. If we understand what people truly *desire*, we can sell it to them.

And tastes don't just differ by geography. They shift with time, just as societies do.

The flavors we now consider classic are relatively recent inventions. Cookies 'n cream was invented by two dairy science students at South Dakota State University in 1979. In the Victorian era they had a taste for cucumbers and fruits and flowers in their ice cream. No longer.

My prized salted caramel is an even more recent addition to the pantheon: 2008 is when it skyrocketed into our consciousness. Remember your history: that's the year the stock market in the US crashed.

Now, why might that be? I don't see coincidence. I see the *trend*.

My analysis is that people were jaded. They wanted that sharpness along with their sugar. They wanted the salt of tears. They wanted a treat that bit back.

I theorize that the events, the societal sea changes, we cannot process in our normal daily lives make their way out as cravings. See: the urge for sour, fermented flavors by the millennial generation whose dreams of home ownership, regular employment, and financial solvency had been left out to curdle in the sun. So, sales of kimchi, sauerkraut, and tart Greek frozen yogurt soared.

Our world is changing; the pantheon is in flux. We cannot cling to the flavors of the past. There's big money to be made in predicting where to look *next*: what the next mover-and-shaker tastemaker flavor will be.

For ice cream is not a thing of the past, though some of this weekend's vaunted experts would have you think so. I'm not here to talk about gloom and doom. I'm not here to talk about the honey bee. I'm not here to talk about the cocoa farms, or vanilla, or refrigeration technology. I am here to point a way forward. I'm here to talk about how tastes change over time. Crisis doesn't just affect our lives and livelihood, it changes our palates.

And that's what I'm here to share with you today. The future. I'm here to teach you how to be ahead of the curve, to anticipate, to invest appropriately. Let us turn then, to the real question: What do people want *now*?

Right now, people want penance.

Our survey data, which you can see behind me, indicates that the unprecedented wildfires correlate with a rise in desire for flavors with a smokey profile and an acrid crunch. The burnt.

Imagine blackened waffle. Imagine overdone toast. Singed marshmallow. It's not such a stretch. I bet you find yourself craving those tastes right now. I bet they offer comfort.

And what do we have in surplus? Charcoal. As the prices of vanilla and honey soar, we might as well use some of this excess. Eat the lost rainforests, savor the old growth.

There is precedent. In many cultures, widows eat the ashes of their beloved. In many cultures "ashes in your mouth" means great disappointment and disillusion. The world is in mourning. Consider Psalms 102:9, "For I have eaten ashes like bread and mingled my drink with weeping."

We, my fellow dairy treat manufacturers, have a chance to be of service to the world, to help its citizens mourn. To pay their respects.

As it gets hotter, people will only want ice cream more. As it gets scarier, they'll seek out the comfort of the ice cream shop. And as the world burns, they'll want to eat the ash, to buy a moment of atonement by the sweet scoop, the pint, or the gallon.

Local Specialty

THE FOG IS unreasonable—thick and too chilly for summer—on my morning bike ride to Bertha's Breakfast Buffet, where I'm lead server and manager. When I cross the bridge to town, it feels like I'm about to roll right off the edge of the map. I edge closer to the center of the lane.

A car swings out of the fog. By the time I see it, it's honking and swerving, clipping my backpack.

I screech to the side. I flip off the car, but it's already sunk back into the gray.

Then a much deeper honking, baritone, comes up from underneath me, like the earth is honking back at that Lexus asshole, taking my side. The sound shakes the bridge.

A tanker—close.

The big ship slinks out from the fog. It's like a cathedral has snuck up next to me: a building bigger than any in town. Massive, wide, tall, and red, with condensation rolling down its immense facade. The tanker is so big it fills my field of vision. There's some foreign script that makes me think of Cyrillic, almost.

I stop pedaling to stare. I've always liked the tankers.

They come from so far away—Panama, the Marshall Islands, Liberia—farther away than I've ever been. I scan the rusty castle of the tanker, looking for someone to wave to. There—on a deck so high it's almost lost in the fog—a few skinny sailors are waving back. I can't make out their expressions, but they are swinging their arms in perfect unison, so perfect it almost looks like a dance. Maybe they are all listening to the same song; only I don't hear any music.

Swish, swish, swish.

I match their cadence; it's easy. In fact, it's almost irresistible. I don't speak their language, so this feels like the least I can do. *Swish, swish, swish: You're stuck in your dead-end job, and I'm stuck in mine, halfway around the world.* But for a moment, we acknowledge each other.

The tanker turns into the narrow channel leading to the port, and disappears again. The sailors are still waving as I lose sight of them.

I've lingered too long already. I kick off.

• • •

I aim to get to Bertha's first, lock my bike, unlock the door, punch in the alarm code, and start three pots of coffee brewing. From 6:00 a.m. to 7:00—the hour before customers—is my favorite part of each day. Cesar, our high school–aged cook, says I am a misanthrope. He's probably right. The restaurant without people in it is so lovely. It will spend the rest of the day devolving into ruin: syrup on the floors, home-fries grime under my fingernails, running out of raspberries.

I refill the ketchup bottles and pickles from our supply in the basement. I pull the butter tabs out of the freezer to defrost on the counter. I'm twenty-six, and I don't remember when but my life has become pocket-size: just something I carry with me on my routines, shrunk down by wage labor and rising rent. I peek at it every once in a while before tucking it away again. Back to work. Maybe I should find my way onto a tanker, stow away, and reinvent myself in the Southern Hemisphere.

Cesar arrives at 6:50. He nods to me without taking off his massive headphones, lights the griddle, and makes me a breakfast sandwich just how I like it: Canadian bacon, charred English muffin, melted American cheese. "It takes three nations to make your perfect sandwich," he joked once. It took me a minute.

Cesar is *smart*. He has a favorite poet, and he remembers every regular's order. He invented a new dish: Eggs Cesar, which is poached eggs over basil and green peppers and cornmeal cakes. He never gets flustered by a rush—he *enjoys* the puzzle of negotiating twelve orders at once, all with different cook times. He's working at Bertha's to save up for his freshman year at UNH. I'm glad he has a plan: someone like Cesar shouldn't get stuck here.

Cesar puts my sandwich in the window and rings the bell, even though it's just us.

It's 7:00. While I've been going through my routines, the coffee's finished brewing. Three dark crystal balls are swirling and simmering. I have to unlock the doors.

Jules and his husband, Cristian, are waiting in the alley. No surprises there. They spend their summers here; seasonal regulars. Jules and Cristian aren't even that much older than me, but they're in Brooks Brothers while I'm in a washed-thin Siouxsie and the Banshees T-shirt.

"Did you hear? Literally or figuratively?" Jules asks me. He's an adjunct professor at one of the Boston schools. He and Cesar would have a lot to talk about, if Cesar could ever get out of the kitchen.

"What?" I ask.

"A tanker hit, ran up on the rocks in the fog. We heard the boom from our rental."

My tanker, my sailors. I picture them waving. I hope they are okay.

"They suspect a spill," says Cristian.

"A spill of what?" I ask.

They give me a funny look. Probably this is a dumb question. Fuel, right? But I read a story once of a molasses spill, and another where a container ship dumped Nikes all over the coast of Washington. I could use a new pair of shoes.

Jules shrugs. "I guess we'll find out. Coffees?"

"Coming up."

Soon, the 9:00 a.m. rush shoves aside my thoughts of the tanker. The other staff clock in and get to work. I'm taking orders and clearing dishes and wiping spills and refilling coffees and brewing more and running back to the window every time Cesar rings the bell. All smiling: at the end of the day, my cheeks will be sore.

Bertha's vibe is small-town and quaint, like a place frozen in time. Except that we've changed immensely. Now that tourists from Boston and beyond have discovered the town, we charge them as much as we can get away with for muffins and scrambles. No one local comes anymore. The tourists take photos with the lobster traps on the ceiling.

Our hollandaise is made from a powder. I've sworn Cesar to secrecy.

The owner lives out of town—cheaper for him that way—and only comes by every month or so to check on things.

I tried a few other things, driving deliveries and dinghy tours of the port. But, with tips, I make as much as my friend who teaches elementary school, and she has student debt and a master's. With rents going up, Bertha's is enough to keep me afloat, barely.

Around 10:00 a.m., we hear sirens and see red flashing lights through Bertha's big front glass windows. Everyone pauses for a moment to watch, forks hovering over their plates. Then we go back to our roles. I laugh at the tourists' jokes and give them directions from their Airbnb to the beach access.

"No lobster?" The customer at table eight gestures past me with his menu, toward the specials chalkboard. He sounds affronted.

"Sorry, all out," I say. What I don't say is that our coast is one of the fastest warming places on the planet. Tourists don't want to hear all that. It's a downer. We'd love to serve lobster, but locally caught are rare and expensive. I can't even remember the last time I had a lobster roll. It'd be like eating dollar bills. Nothing tastes that good. "But our special benedict today is fiddleheads."

"Fiddleheads? What's that?"

"Local specialty!" I say. "Imagine asparagus. Delicious. Seasonal and grown locally."

"Organic?"

"Of course."

On the specials board I've drawn fiddleheads as little green swirls, like the tentacles of a sea monster.

"Sure. Why not?" He leans into his wife. "Something exotic."

I smile. I hope he thinks I'm laughing with him.

Fiddleheads are a fern. They look fancy. I think they taste nasty: bitter and slimy. But they make for a great Instagram photo: green swirl peeking out from underneath a yellow yolk. Proof someone went on a trip.

In season we can get fiddleheads for cheap, fifteen dollars a pound, then drizzle some hollandaise and smoked paprika on them and charge that much for a single plate. No local would pay that much for a fiddlehead; they'd laugh in your face. Fiddleheads are a shibboleth; Cesar taught me that word last week. He's studying for his SATs.

"Is Bertha around?" the customer asks.

"She's out today!" I say. "Just missed her!"

As far as I know, there never was a Bertha. The closest thing we have is the mascot hanging on our wooden sign above the door: a crusty mermaid holding a carved spatula, flipping some bacon. Her paint is chipping.

· · ·

Bertha's closes at three. I want to go see the tanker, but an exasperating party walks in the door around 2:50. They take their time; they order mimosas. I'm finally rid of them around four. Half an hour later I split the tips and wave bye to Cesar. "See you here tomorrow." *Same thing over again.*

By the time I'm finally free to bike over to the wreck, most everyone has left. The tanker is still in the water, a little off-kilter, a little too nestled in the rocks. There are wide, thin nets trying to keep in— what? Some contaminants I can't see. It smells like cinnamon and paint thinner.

Next to me a seagull coughs. I didn't know they could do that. Everything is poisoned, probably: the rocks, the air, the water. Sayonara to the few lobsters that are left. That seagull's days are numbered.

There's the WMUR News 9 van, filming some footage for the evening news. I get a funny idea and I swing my bike and my body into their shot, between the camera and the tanker in the background. I start waving my arms in the same slow rhythm of the sailors from earlier that morning. *Swish, swish, swish.* I don't know why I do this. Just—I have this idea that the sailors might be watching. I picture them in the ER, wrapped in those thin silver blankets they give marathoners and bombing victims, here in this cruel foreign country where no one speaks their language. I want them to know that I remember them, that I'm worried about them.

While I'm waving, I hear the reporter mention the yacht.

"A yacht in the shipping lane." He says the tanker swerved to avoid the yacht, and BOOM. That's what caused the wreck and the spill of Lord knows what. A fucking yacht.

Just a playground to the tourists. But we live here. It's our livelihood and our home. Most of my friends from high school have already been priced out. I'm barely hanging on.

I get jittery with anger. But what am I gonna do? There's no bad guy to fight. I just keep waving. Up and down, up and down. The reporter tries to scare me away, but I bike a little farther and keep waving, *swish, swish, swish.* I won't let them get a clean shot. They'll have to use what they got.

· · ·

Soon the tanker is towed away. On TV, local marine biologists are concerned and local environmental activists are enraged, but mostly, life goes back to normal. "We won't know the long term effects till . . ." The news stories slow. I add the yacht and the crash and the spill to my register of simmering offenses. I go back to my routines.

Except on one of my morning rides into Bertha's, I do see something along the ocean road. Around 5:20, a black van with no windows is parked with its back to the water. A couple of men on walkie-talkies are standing next to the van with their ties blowing into their faces. They are watching scuba divers in fancy all-black gear walk backward into the water, *step, step, step,* carefully over the slippery rocks.

I keep biking, no time to stop. But I glance over at them. The divers sink under. I'm happy—someone is going to do something to fight the spill. To look after the waters.

As I pass right by them I can see into the van, a little, just for a second. I see a speargun, as tall as me. The image lodges in my brain like a splinter, but I can't be late. I'm the one with the keys to Bertha's, and there's no way I'll leave Cesar waiting for me in the alley.

· · ·

Every once in a while, as summer's beachcombers turn to fall's leaf peepers, I think again of the tanker and the spill and the sailors and the strange van. But it's not till winter, when the town empties out and business turns slow, that Cesar and I go to the shore together.

All Cesar's studying paid off. He got a scholarship to UNH. But every weekend day he's still at Bertha's frying eggs. He's got to save up for books and food and housing.

One of those weekend days is so unbelievably slow that we've already sent the dishwasher home. We make pyramids out of the red plastic cups; up to six levels high before they tumble down. I wash the front windows and Cesar cleans behind the stove—all the bottom-of-the-list tasks. Cesar films us taking shots of hot sauce and horseradish, and we stand in the kitchen counting the likes and reading the comments to each other. Still no customers.

"Can we get out of here?" Cesar asks.

Well, why not? We're not making any real money today.

I write, "Gone fishing," on the back of a paper placemat and tape it to the front door. We grab our jackets.

Cesar stands on the back of my bike; it's not far to the shore. At first I was embarrassed to tell him I didn't have a car, but he's always been cool about it. "Very eco-conscious of you," he said.

We find a cove to hide us from the road and settle in to watch the lapping waves against the rocks and smoke blunts for a while. It is overcast and chilly, but that means no one else is around. Our cove shields us from the wind.

I sit far away enough from Cesar to make it clear that I'm not hitting on him or trying to get him too high or anything. I've met enough creeps in my life to be wary of acting like them. Cesar's clever enough, I hope, to avoid the traps I fell into, to get out of this town, clever enough that if he's choosing to spend this free day in my company, then maybe I'm not so bad after all.

The weed is kicking in and I'm having all these nice syrupy thoughts. Despite the cold, it is cozy, nestled into the rocks. I'm thinking that the way Cesar trusts me makes me want to earn that trust, to be a better type of person. Cesar doesn't think I'm a fuckup. I'm getting dangerously close to saying this corny shit out loud to Cesar, so I look out at the water instead.

"Hold up," Cesar says. He points over my shoulder.

I turn around. It's just a lobster, on the rock above and behind me.

"Little buddy must be stoned too," I say.

That makes Cesar laugh.

It's not normal to see one so close, or so far away from the tide.

"Hey, there's another." I point to a rock in the distance. A lobster is waving its antennae around and looking a little lost.

Like one of those Magic Eye pictures, now that I've seen two, I see them everywhere. What I notice first is all the antennae, each attached to its own lobster, tapping out the same beat, like a metronome, up and down, in sync. There must be twenty, no, forty—more. We are surrounded. Some are between us and the bike, which I left back up near the road. Some are near and some are far. Every third rock or so has a lobster on it. Blue-black and chunky, gnarled. The same color and slickness as the rocks around them. And those antennae: bouncing along to some beat they can hear that we don't, some lobster frequency.

"I thought the ones that were left had died off after the spill," Cesar says. He is staring out at them and frowning. He starts rubbing his hands, like to warm them, in the same rhythm as the antennae. Does he notice?

"Not these ones," I say.

"I guess not."

"Maybe they're special. Hey, man, don't fuck with it," I tell Cesar, but he is already bending down to pick up the closest one by the tail. Maybe I'm high; maybe I'm paranoid—but my stomach clenches. Cesar is smart, but I have this feeling that is a real dumb idea.

"I just want a closer look," he says.

The lobster Cesar is reaching for is just sitting there twitching. Then it scurries, but not away—*toward* Cesar.

Wrong again. Something is wrong.

On every rock, the lobsters start moving at the same time. One single lobster crawling on a rock barely makes a sound. But all of them, at once, is loud: close and fast.

Next thing I know, my pants and sleeves are heavy, and wet. I stand up and lobsters are swinging from my clothes by their pincers. I'm kicking and shaking while I scramble on the rocks toward Cesar. I don't want them to touch my bare hands or my face.

Cesar is a step ahead of me, rushing out of the cove and back toward the bike. In his rushing he missteps. He catches himself with his hands against the rocks; doesn't hit his head, but the lobsters crawl onto his arms from all sides, over each other. I slap one off his shoulder; I hoist him back on his feet. Another one is climbing up his leg. Fuck. I grab it by its tail and fling it back toward the water.

We've got to get away; we can't keep swatting at them. There's too many. For every one we fight off, three more crawl up behind it. We have to run.

"Go!" I yell to Cesar. If we can make it to the bike, we'll be out of here. We can't stop moving, even to shrug them off. They're acting like a swarm, like ants or bees. Coordinated attack. Their carapaces crunch, sturdy under my sneakers. From a distance we must look mad; high-stepping and kicking and flailing our arms, trying to shake them off, wave after wave. Thank god for the bike. When I throw one leg over, there are still some lobsters hanging off of me, but I start pushing my weight into the pedals.

"Get on!"

Cesar doesn't need convincing. He's on, hugging my shoulders and panting.

We take off, still hauling a half dozen lobsters, clinging to us like ugly brooches.

I push us into the cold wind, away from that cove. I don't look back. But Cesar does.

"They're still coming."

"For real?"

"They won't catch us, but they're coming."

None of this is how lobsters act.

As soon as the cove and swarm are out of sight, I pull over under some bare trees. I rip off my jacket. It's frigid and my arms and legs are wet, but I can't stand to have those things on me one more second.

"Fuck was that?" Cesar asks me.

We're still on the bicycle. My jacket is squirming on the ground where they—two of them—are trapped in the folds. I step off the bike, willing myself to go toward them. I raise my boot to stomp the whole situation, but Cesar says:

"Wait."

"What?"

"Just a minute."

So I wait. The jacket and what's inside it twitch on the ground. A clueless car rips past.

We catch our breath.

. . .

Cesar convinces me to bring the bundle of freak lobsters and jacket back to Bertha's. For a "test."

"They're weird, right?" he says.

"Yeah. But I don't want to touch them."

"I'll hold them," he says, and he does, cradling my wet jacket the whole way back, tight.

Back at Bertha's, Cesar sets up these experiments while I brew coffee.

We dump one in a cardboard box and another in a trash bin, a room apart. When he kicks the trash can, the one in the box shudders. Some strange solidarity. Cesar's looking at it like a scientist, but I'm staring at the lobster in the box, on the floor of our kitchen, and a different idea comes to me.

"What do you think it tastes like?" I ask.

"What, are you gonna try some?" Cesar says.

"No—not me." We've bested them once. We could do it again.

Cesar is frowning, thinking.

I fill the quiet: "The brunch crowd. It won't hurt anybody. Probably."

Finally, Cesar says, "These lobsters are doing fine. Better even, than before."

"Right."

"Like super lobster."

"A health food!"

. . .

It takes us a few weeks, but we figure it out.

We go back to the cove. I've never seen them anywhere else, but we find them at the cove every time. We try the lobster traps from the ceiling, once, but that doesn't work without a boat. Eventually we figure out a way to swoop a dozen of them on a single trip. We use my bike and some gear from Bertha's—milk crate, kitchen trash bag, broom. Cesar hangs off the back of my bike. He holds tight to the trash bag, which squirms with a sickly rhythm, like one big heartbeat.

At Bertha's we store them in the basement, each in its own bucket of cold water, each with something heavy on top: a crate of tomatoes or a sack of potatoes.

By summer we've got it down to a routine. A new routine. One that makes the world seem bigger, not smaller. Lobster's back on the menu at Bertha's.

I slip down into the basement to pull one from its bucket. All of them snap at me in lazy unison, their mystical beat.

Upstairs I pass it to Cesar; he stabs it in the middle of the forehead. Once it's cooked, white and pink and covered in butter and hollandaise, you'd never know it was any different.

I sprinkle some parsley on top and head out onto the floor. It's only 10:30. We've already sold fourteen plates of the lobster benedict, at $19.99 a plate before any tip, and we aren't paying a cent for the meat.

We are making a killing, pure profit, under the table. We're catching the lobsters ourselves. The owner doesn't know a thing about it; we're pocketing the profit: Cesar's idea. He said to me, "Those things you want for me, I want them for you too, man." So we're splitting it fifty-fifty, the extra work and the extra profit. There's no deliveries to check off, everything's off the books. Cesar will have his college fund, and then some; I'm saving to get out. That's as far as I know. Bertha's isn't forever anymore.

No one retches; no one shivers. No one's eyes roll back in their head. Only, I swear to Cesar, later, as we're closing up shop that day, that there was this moment when everyone who ordered the special reached for their napkin. They unfolded it slowly, one, two, three, and wiped their mouths, left to right. Then they set it back down on their lap, all at once, in perfect unison.

The Disgrace of the Commodore

THE COMMODORE deduces that he is in purgatory. There are certain clues: daylessness, nightlessness, the lack of escape. His accommodation, a small wooden room, is just too short to stand up in, just too narrow to lay down in properly. It is rather like a coffin.

He recognizes this room. He knows her smell of camphor: a hold in the belly of his ship. He recognizes her exact creaking when he places his palms against her paneling. He can intuit the whole of her, from the spritsail to the stern lantern.

She bucks; she is at sea. Some strange sea of the afterlife.

He places his ear to the wall: he is not alone. The great ghost ship is crowded with footsteps, with hollers and whispers. He has tried yelling, but no one seems to hear, let alone heed his commands. After all, he surrendered this ship, long ago. After the British took her, she was parceled out as lumber into the English countryside.

• • •

She was beautiful. Thirty-eight guns, three masts, like a greyhound on the water. Her rigging practically sang, at once a refuge and a weapon, a sloop of war, a pride of the US Navy.

In 1807 she was ambushed just outside her port of Norfolk. The British boarded. It only took a few minutes.

"You see," he'd testified at his court martial, "we'd only just taken on a new dog. It was her first time at sea. The spaniel, Lucy, was frightened of the cannons. I thought she would not be so scared if the British and I just talked among ourselves. None of the boys would be killed. No shots."

His peers were unmoved. This was not the reasoning of a commander. He was stripped of his title, branded a coward, and exiled to Copenhagen, with its narrow streets, flat pastries, pervading chill. The Commodore worked to excise the damned softness within himself. He took bracing walks alone along the canals. If they gave him another chance, he would be different, better.

Now he finds his surrendered ship returned to him, or rather he to it, ensnared within her dark bowels.

• • •

The Commodore has benefited from a fine classical education; he knows that purgatory traffics in ironies. The imbeciles manning this ghost ship are his descendants, generations and generations down. Muddled sounds sift to him through the boards. They are muttering just beyond his walls, a miscegenational, foulmouthed, shameless brood. He hears them playing tenpins in the halls: thunderous crashes and brash laughter.

They are picnicking on the upper deck; they are smoking sweet cigarettes out of the portholes. They race through the galley; they dry out their unmentionables on the mizzenmast, in the salt air. They inhabit every corner of his ship, grubbing up its gloss with their fingers.

. . .

With him in his little room is his massive bicorne hat. The Commodore remembers a certain grandchild, Samuel, who often sat on his knee. For little Samuel, the Commodore would put on this hat and amuse the boy by crossing his eyes and puffing out his cheeks.

. . .

His descendants are throwing things overboard: his locket containing an illustration of his Suzette's brown eye, a rope bed, his tobacco pipe, his cage-handled rapier. He hears the splashing but can do nothing to stop them. He paces the small room.

The Commodore imagines that his present confinement is a test, one he might pass, and thereby escape. His descendants—their mockery, their overeducated women, their unholy unions, their unbecoming leisure—are dark ghosts of the future yet to come. He might yet avoid them. He is learning his lesson. He will awaken, younger yet wiser, and will not surrender his ship this time.

. . .

His brass spyglass goes over the side of the ghostly ship. He remembers Samuel as a boy once picked it up and tried to hoist it clumsily to his eye. The Commodore had snatched it away, placed it on a high shelf. It might have gotten broken. "If we are to have anything to pass down, it must be carefully preserved."

The boy always seemed a little afraid of him after that.

. . .

There is running in the halls of the ghost ship. He hears wood splinter-ing. His descendants are hacking the ship to pieces. The Commodore backs into a corner of his little wooden room. They are carrying her away. The Commodore spits. He takes off his boots and throws them at the wall. He puts his hot face in his hands. They will set him adrift, if he does not simply drown. He'd rather remain in this tight small room.

He will fight them. He will protect what is his, what little is left.

. . .

A strange chime draws the Commodore from his corner. Behind the terrifying chopping sounds and irreverent laughter he hears the tinkling of wine glasses. A wedding speech. They are saying his name; some namesake of the Commodore is getting married.

The Commodore leans into the wall; he holds his breath. They are telling the famous story of his surrender. The voice tells of the baring of his ship's beams, their reassembly into a pub in a small English village. Decades pass, England changes, the pub remains.

A new voice takes up the story; a woman is speaking now. Her family moved from India to that small English village. She recounts the pub, the swinging sign, the beer scent wafting out of a red door. And how could she have known that she'd meet and fall in love with this descendant, the namesake of the man who surrendered the ship?

The audience laughs, what a happy coincidence. The laughter seems tender. This is only the beginning of the couple's story. His own is just a footnote in theirs. The Commodore laughs a little himself, too. It is a nice story.

. . .

The descendants grow closer. They are singing as they work. To them this ship is wood. It might become a table or a cradle or a bookshelf or a house where they will raise children.

The Commodore remembers his surrender, but this time not the glowering of his straight-backed peers at his trial. Rather, he remembers the nuzzle of Lucy's wet nose; he remembers taking off his military hat and putting it on Samuel's small head.

He takes a deep breath, tasting the stale air of his hold. They are coming, his children's children he has never met. They are almost here. The ship is already theirs. All he can control is how he meets them, the timbre if not the terms of his surrender. What's left is just a formality. And he's always loved a ceremony.

The Commodore stands up in his little room and prepares himself. He takes off his hat and cradles it in his hands, fluffs the dirty plumes. He's practiced this all before.

They are just outside the wall now, slicing and cracking and hauling. There comes a breeze through the slats of his chamber. It smells of salt and open air. He will surrender the ship, only let him shake their hands just once. He cannot imagine what monstrous, new thing they will build with her bones. He cannot imagine. Perhaps he will get to see.

Tiger on My Roof

BECAUSE I WAS A coward, I skipped Dee's funeral. I told myself I'd already sat in the pews and mourned too many children. I knew how these funerals went, how I went at them. Kayla, shot at a house party. The ambulance was too slow. Erick, shot at the bus stop his senior year. Damian, who was just a freshman. Four students shot and killed during my seven years teaching woodshop at Auburn Academy. Dee was the last.

At Dee's funeral there would be wailing and crying and music and words, all of it insufficient, impotent, too late. Too many families, too many mothers I never met until that moment, and how do you introduce yourself, then? "I'm Mr. Orie; I taught Dee twice a week for his woodshop elective." Past tense. His final project never finished.

I bought a somber plum tie for my first funeral—Kayla, in my second year of teaching. At the church a freshman put a slender arm around my shoulder; I was crying so hard, so loudly and red-faced. I think the kid was embarrassed for me. I was one of the only white people there; I think all the white people were Auburn teachers. I was embarrassed for myself, to be taking up so much space, bringing attention to my own grief. Or perhaps I should have been louder, shouting and railing. We were supposed to protect children. As adults, as teachers, isn't that our job? The contract: "Trust me, do what I say, and I will protect you and guide you and steward you into adulthood. You will have an adulthood. It will all make sense then."

That tie became my funeral tie. I never wanted to touch it again. I was more comfortable admiring the murals—the faces of the young but dead, made massive, smiling, in electric colors and surrounded by flowers or other emblems of life and fragility. Always there, always young. I walked by them every day at our high school's campus, before unlocking my classroom door and flicking on the fluorescent lights, usually before dawn.

• • •

It was fourteen years ago that I skipped Dee's funeral, then ran away from teaching. Dee's death had gotten to me more than the first three. Perhaps his death hit me harder because my son, Jacob, had come into my life, had begun walking and grabbing at the world around him. I had known the other kids better, had grieved. Maybe if I'd known Dee better, I would have known where to put the rage. Or maybe it had just been one too many deaths, and I had tapped out, uselessly.

It's one thing to have the unthinkable happen once. It's another to have it happen over and over, for it to become very thinkable, very familiar, to expect it. When text messages would arrive at unexpected hours, I would begin to tense, not even wondering what had happened, just *Who? Who is it this time?*

Dove emojis, "REST IN POWER" on social posts. A twenty-year-old Auburn Academy grad posting, "This one surprised me. This one got me." *This one*. I know what he means.

The papers talked about the violence in that neighborhood as an epidemic. I worried Jacob might catch it, somehow, from me. Logically, I knew he was safe, but the grief felt big, sticky, sneaky. So I retreated. It was so easy to leave. Easy to leave that school, that neighborhood. My students and their families didn't have that choice. But I did, and I took it. My wife, Melissa, was relieved when I resigned. Her income floated us a few months while I spent my days with Jacob and reoriented my life.

Now Jacob is a teenager. Tonight, he is out far too late, which means I am lying awake in bed. I have been thinking that every siren is for him. I think of Jacob's pale belly peeking out of his too-short T-shirts, as he grows too tall, too fast. I am proud of how he is growing up. He is generally kind and clever. I know, logically, that he is not likely to be killed. I hate that I know this because he is white, he is middle class, he lives in a different zip code (just two over) from Auburn Academy. I am grateful for it, the safety. I am enraged by it, that he is safe when my Auburn kids were not. Jacob gets to be a little dumb. If Jacob died, it would make the front page. Dee's death didn't.

Instead of waiting in the dark for Jacob to get home, I pick up my phone and I go looking for the tiger.

• • •

Dee had been found before dawn. The local news said, "Two adolescents, maroon Ford, both unresponsive." The police statement said, "Death by gunshot." There would be further investigation, but I didn't have hope that any of the questions that mattered—Why? How could you? What could be worth it? Why Dee?—would be answered.

• • •

The day of Dee's funeral, I washed my car instead. Slowly, meticulously. Layer after layer of soap, washing away. I sprayed the suds into the storm drain. My mind snagged on all the little wrongnesses—pollen on the windshield, mud splatters, paint scratches—in an effort to not confront the big wrong: the child gone.

• • •

A week after Dee's funeral, I found myself driving half an hour out to the intersection where Dee's body was found, Poplar Street and Near-water Ave, to see the dedication of his memorial. I had left Melissa at home to watch Jacob. He was a toddler, still too young. Melissa only sighed when I left, which meant she was worried about me but did not want to interfere. Other spots around town had wreaths or concrete Buddhas or helium balloons tied to chain link fences, marking drive-by deaths with bits of color and affection: infusions of memory into the landscape. I figured grief might enter me more easily if I had some art piece to bounce my thoughts off of. Just me and the monument. But there was already a crowd gathered. "Virtual," the social media graphic had said. "Alternate reality." "Interactive."

I wasn't sure what to expect. There was no physical marker, but a haphazard line of cars with their noses nestled into the levee hill made it obvious. Otherwise it was just open air. A kind of monument you'd only find if you knew to look for it.

At the intersection a scattering of people milled around in a rough circle. It wasn't a busy intersection, but every so often a car honked its way through, the driver looking around confused. The crowd of mourners parted, briefly, only to recollapse into each other when the way was cleared. Some other teachers at the edges nodded to each other. A handful of kids from school stood in a circle in matching memorial T-shirts—blue spray paint swirls and angel's wings. The teachers watched them to understand how to act, everything all muddled. How unfair to them, to have to teach us.

The kids pointed their phones toward the intersection, so we did, too. They stood on their tiptoes or ducked around each other to track something. One girl, who looked about twelve, waved an arm around in disbelief, trying to stroke something. Her other arm held her pink phone out to scope what she was reaching toward.

Through my phone's camera it became visible: a yellow grassy hill sat where none was in reality, enveloping the intersection where Dee had been shot, where the SUV had skidded off the road, where the crime scene tape had already been put up and taken down. On the hill, eight or nine white tigers were lounging. Some were cubs; some had low swinging bellies. Some were standing, some reclining with amused eyes. They flicked their tails. They panted; they shook their massive necks.

A breeze that we didn't feel pushed the savannah grasses of the tigers' hill. It was a neat trick.

A kid about sixteen—Dee's age—made like he was going to try to climb the hill. But when he got close enough, he was swallowed into it, disappearing from view. At least that's how it looked on my screen. After a moment he wandered out on the other side of the intersection. I heard someone asking what he saw in there, but I was too far away to hear. And I didn't want to get too close to the tigers.

One of the pack had begun to prowl, walking the border of the hill where it took a sharp bank down toward the ground. Pacing and showing his teeth—looking right into the eyeline of our phone cameras. He snarled at me. I stepped back. What a feat of artistic programming, to predict how people would behave, to manufacture an illusion of spontaneous interaction: to have the tigers seem to see us, react to us, maneuver around us. I wondered how long till the animation would loop.

A car sped by. I felt a metal sinking feeling. I froze; I flinched. I'd heard of people shooting up memorials here before. But the car just kept going, turned the corner, and someone shouted something illegible out of the window, a burn or a tribute, impossible to say. No one else seemed to react. Another reminder: I was a coward.

A woman, who looked to be about twenty, with long heavy braids, started singing, impromptu: "Amazing Grace." Many people hummed along or swayed, some lowering their phones. Others continued to watch the tigers. The tigers didn't seem to hear. They scratched behind their ears. They looked out at us.

· · ·

A few days after visiting the memorial, I opened the camera app to photograph a lumber receipt. I cleared away Jacob's stuffed animals and set the receipt against the oak kitchen table. I was met by a massive pair of dark carnivore eyes.

"Shit!" I threw the phone at the threat. It bounced on the linoleum. Nothing was there. I took deep breaths. Everything was still, empty. Just kitchen.

I stooped to pick my phone back up. Melissa came over to see why I had yelled. With her looking over my shoulder, I reopened the camera. First, I pointed it away from the kitchen, toward our front door.

Nothing.

When I swiveled the camera back toward the receipt and the table, though, what had startled me was now clearer. Peeking over the table, toward us: flaring nostrils, the top half of a white tiger's face. He was tall enough to look at us right over the tabletop. Through the table and chair legs we could see his mass, stretching and collapsing with breath, his muscular hindquarters.

"Jesus," said Melissa, laughing and hesitant.

"Yeah."

"Did he follow you home?" Melissa asked. I'd told her about the memorial, in our bed, in the dark. Just the concrete details. She'd wrapped her arms around me.

I smirked at this idea. "I guess?"

"How cool."

At first I thought this was a laugh, maybe a glitch, a bug, if an intricate and beautiful one, like when my avatar in a videogame walks out onto the empty sky or gets trapped halfway into a wall.

But my tiger persisted.

I followed the tiger as it loped up our staircase. Another day I caught it rolling lazily on the carpet. The AR was more sophisticated than I had thought at first. The tiger explored our house and chose favorite spots. I could reliably find him lying flat under our coffee table, though he was so big that his paws and tail jutted out onto the carpet. Did everyone who went to Dee's memorial come home with a tiger in their phone, projected into their home and daily routines? Did their tigers snarl at them, too?

. . .

In those first few months after Dee died, when I wasn't sleeping much at night—my thoughts tumbling without insight, scrolling and lurking and laying one hand on the lump of Melissa, phone turned away so the light would not bother her—I sometimes got out of bed to look for the tiger.

On one of the first nights I went looking for him, I turned on the camera app in the dark; the world was a warm staticky red gray. If the tiger were asleep, he could be very hard to find. But I thought he was probably a nocturnal hunter. So he'd be awake too.

I pointed it at the foot of the bed, as if the tiger were a loyal pet. Of course, he was not there.

I wandered out of the bedroom and into the hall.

That's where the camera caught his sentinel eyes, peering at me from behind the bookshelf full of melamine plates. His eyes were very still, gleaming like jewels in his dark silhouette, which was barely visible, just a pool of greater darkness.

He was motionless; only his nostrils flaring slightly. Tensed, about to pounce. I stood paralyzed, wanting to run, though I knew he could not hurt me. He'd spotted me. My breath was quick and shallow. I clicked the side of my phone to shut the camera off. I was alone in the empty hall. I leaned against the wall and breathed in deep.

. . .

Jacob took naturally to the tiger, figured it out quickly. Perhaps he was already used to friends and miracles appearing in the small periscope of my phone's screen. He'd tug at my pocket and ask to take my phone out and go tiger hunting. He'd hold the phone as he ran forward or drop it and I'd have to go and wipe it clean of playground mulch, the camera app still on. Curious, I'd swing the phone around till I sighted the white tiger, lying under the swings, lazily batting just a little too slowly at the children, and scrunching his nose as they swung just out of reach.

At our place, the tiger played hide-and-seek. He'd turn up impossibly in a kitchen cabinet, bisected by a plank of wood that his algorithm had decided for some reason not to mind, or standing on his hind legs licking at the spot where water might have been running from a showerhead. Jacob would laugh and laugh and go stand in the empty shower too. "Found him!" he'd shriek.

There's a photo I took of Jacob on one of our summer day trips out to Ship Island where the tiger is squeezed into the frame next to him, squinting into the sun, panting, with his fangs out. His fangs are as big as Jacob's four-year-old hands. They are almost posing together: Jacob looking up at the camera because I've said his name, butt on the ground, digging for clams. Jacob's face and the tiger's face are almost touching, though they don't see each other. Something in the tiger's programming knows how to make him graze people, hover right next to them, keep the illusion up. It has perfected the use of negative space.

Those days, almost every time I opened my phone's camera, it was to point it at Jacob. Photos of him climbing oak trees featured the tiger, weightless, lounging on a branch above. A tiger swimming behind him in the neighborhood swimming pool. At Disney World, the tiger sniffing Goofy's asshole, perplexed. Batting at fish in the Georgia Aquarium. I used to send my sister photos of Jacob constantly; to avoid her questions, I began to crop the tiger out. The resulting photos had awkward slices of stripes, or muzzle, or tail, indistinguishable to most people but clear to me: the tiger stalking him, stalking me.

When Jacob won bronze at his third-grade science fair, the tiger sat behind him in the photo, massive, stern faced, ears up. Like some cartoonish family portrait. I couldn't tell if the tiger was guarding Jacob or menacing him. It irked me.

I just didn't want a tiger in every photo of my kid. I had not asked for this. I'd left. I'd left Auburn Academy years ago, but the tiger had followed me, followed Jacob. That might have been when I started thinking of ways to get rid of the tiger.

There seemed to be no way to turn it off. I tried powering the phone all the way down. I tried uninstalling and reinstalling the camera app. I brought it to the local stores, and the clerk, who must have been about Dee's age, looked at me in bafflement.

Sometimes I thought I had outwaited the tiger, that he had moved on. Then a few minutes later I would spot him, embedded in the back tangles of our overgrown garden, his massive form gently squatting to sniff the jasmine.

· · ·

I decided to deposit the tiger back where I had found him. I said I was leaving for lunch, and I drove across town to the intersection of Poplar and Nearwater, where the levee and the road meet.

When I got there, it was empty. A plastic bag drifted by. Cicadas thrummed, and the few cars that passed rolled by so fast that they tugged at the dense air around them. The sun was high and the night's dew was still radiating hot moisture off everything. My tires were loud on the gravel as I pulled over.

Once I parked, I pulled out my phone and checked for my tiger. There he was. He loomed hilariously large in the backseat. If he had breath, he would have been breathing on the back of my neck. The tiger was looking out the window, raising its nose to smell, but the windows were rolled up. Good, it seemed to want to get out of the car, like a dog at the park. *Go*, I thought, *you're released*.

I had wondered whether the memorial would still be up. It was. The tigers were still on the hill, sunning themselves, unconcerned with me. They had not faded or dispersed, despite the lack of viewers.

I looked over the neighborhood around the intersection: small hunched houses with short driveways, scraggly trees, and persistent crabgrass, the trappings of a suburban neighborhood being overtaken by wilderness. Everything was green and wet. The tigers on their dry yellow hill stood out, alien.

They seemed to be sunning themselves, though it was quite cloudy and threatening rain. Whoever had programmed it had made no allow-

ances for weather. The hill and the tigers were awash in otherworldly
light; the grass of the hill was the yellow of the savannah, perpetually.
It felt all wrong, foreign, fake.

This wasn't about Dee at all, I thought. I imagined some trendy young
artist, probably not from here, probably full of self-importance, playing
with the death of a kid he'd never met as a way of flirting with serious-
ness, with gravity, trying to give heft to some preconceived concept
he'd cooked up in Seattle or wherever. The bits of admiration I'd felt
for the memorial turned sour. No art could make Dee's death better,
do enough to mark it. There was no meaning or beauty to be found in
something so ugly, so wrong. It was wrong to try.

My tiger loped away from me, toward his comrades on the yellow
sunlit hill. He opened his mouth wide in a roar; his neck vibrated with
it, but I couldn't hear anything.

· · ·

Would Dee have liked the memorial? He liked big projects, big state-
ments. He must have had a thing for tigers I never knew about. He
was always doodling. I could picture Dee, never sitting still, clearing
his workbench of pine-smelling shavings, his head engulfed in wide
plastic safety goggles that made his dreads poke out mad-scientist-style
above the elastic. His eyes locked to the circular saw while the rest of
him bopped and danced. Someone whispering something to him, and
him shaking his head and laughing: "Nah, breh, it's not like that." His
puppyish tone, a love of being mocked, passing absurd ideas back and
forth with classmates as he made a sloppy box that would never go on
to hold anything at all.

Little bits of overheard conversation. Sometimes that's all I got as a
teacher. That and the pieces he made in class: his wooden bowl among
the other bowls. His shelf had a drip of Ipswich Pine–colored stain
marring it, where he'd applied it too thickly. He hadn't listened to my
warnings. But what did that matter now?

I wished my memories were more substantial, of some significant conversation or mentorship moment. I wish I'd known him better. "Steady," I would tell Dee, "no goofing with your hands so close to the saw." His hands looked tiny in the thick orange safety gloves, engulfed by them. I remember he would flop his gloves around, grinning at how cartoonish they looked.

Dee once showed me a sketch of something he wanted to make in class. I say "something" because it was not clear what it was. It was not functional: not furniture, or shelves, or a box. It was sculptural, perhaps. Composed of many curves. Maybe, if our school had a lathe, then maybe. I tried to explain to him what a lathe was, and that we couldn't afford that. It was clear that Dee's mind was working in a different medium. "Maybe take a pottery class, buddy," I'd told him.

But Dee was stubborn about it and kept trying to build what his mind saw with our standard 2×4s and jigsaw and circular saw. "I saw a video of someone using a chainsaw. You got one of those?" he asked.

"No. And I wouldn't let you touch it if I did."

Dee just laughed at that. Went back to it.

My purview, my scope of time and space with Dee was small. Fourth period, Tuesday and Thursday, 1:30–2:45 p.m. I didn't know much— anything, really—about Dee outside of the times in woodshop. I scolded Dee once for playing with the wood glue, smearing it on his hands to watch it dry before peeling and picking it away. I had warned him not to waste the lumber. What did I know of wastefulness? Dee should not have trusted me. I did nothing to protect him; I imparted no wisdom. He kept trying to use the circular saw to make his curves, and the way I taught him to do that safely was to relentlessly cut the corners off, over and over again, so that he created a curve compiled of many small straight lines. Quick, controlled, safe cuts. I wish I could see his piece, finished. After he died and I skipped his funeral, I tried, once, to write a letter to his mother. I'd wanted to give her that unfinished, untitled project. But I never did. *Who am I?* I thought. *What would I have to share, to say?*

I don't even know what happened to it. I left it in the woodshop closet. I turned in my key. Probably it was tossed out into the dumpster with all the other student work that wasn't brought home.

I hated that I didn't know where Dee's piece had gone, that it had been anonymously cast aside, unfinished; that I hadn't even tried to hold onto it. I only ever saw the drawing, and I never could tell what he was going for. Maybe it didn't translate into two dimensions very well. But Dee could see it.

I should have kept it. It wouldn't have made any difference.

It wouldn't be enough. I should have kept it.

. . .

That day, when I returned to the memorial to ditch the tiger, Dee remained gone. His thoughts were inaccessible.

I realized I could not tell which tiger was mine. I felt nauseous, being so near the tigers but not able to tell which was the one that lived with us in our house, playing hide-and-seek with Jacob. Jacob—Jacob would be furious at me for losing him. I started walking quickly around the hill, holding my phone in front of me, waving it around.

The tigers on the hill looked placidly back at me, or past me, and licked their paws. I tried to compare them through my camera's lens. Was there some familiar mannerism mine had adopted? Was he sticking nearer to me than those others? How could I not know him?

I tried a desperate experiment. I started to walk away from the hill. I went slow. I used the camera's selfie mode to peer over my own shoulder, back at the memorial.

I hoped, and sure enough, one of the tigers watched me go. He stilled, then rose, descended the slope, leaving the gathering of his fellows and the warm unreality to pace after me at a distance of many yards. I was so grateful for his predatory stalk. I couldn't be sure it was the same tiger, but why would it not be? Of course, he couldn't be jettisoned so easily. He got in the car with me. I wanted to put the seat belt on him. But of course, I could not.

. . .

Now I routinely borrow Melissa's phone to photograph finished dressers and consoles and tables, to avoid the befuddling white tigers in my marketing materials. My tiger has followed me across three new phones, syncing along with all my other data. Even when I do use my own camera app to take a picture of something, I sometimes don't even notice the tiger, at first. In the framed photos of our Belize caving trip, just curling into the edge of the photo, a striped black-and-white tail.

. . .

It is 1:38 a.m., and Jacob still hasn't made it back yet. I check his bedroom: no tiger. I pace the hallways.

The tiger has to be here somewhere. I start to look outside. Maybe it is hunting. Exploring.

It is a warm August night. No wonder Jacob wants to be out in it. I push aside the banana plant leaves and look in our backyard. Nothing. I look under the house. I swing open our squeaky iron front gate.

I'm out front when a car pulls up. It is Jacob, home, getting dropped off. His eyes are bleary, his hair is mussy. He might be a little drunk. I wave at the kid who is in the driver's seat.

I think of how the rules are so quickly changing. I used to be furious if Jacob would ever skip class. But now I find myself saying, clumsily: "It's okay to take a day now and then." What I want to tell him is "Do whatever you need to do to get away from what hurts you, to solve the puzzle of staying alive, to find a way." The things that threaten him might be things I can't even see. I worry about depression, drugs, heartache, car accidents. All the things I told Dee would keep him safe did not: the finger safeties on the spinning saw, the gloves, the goggles, the bells, the locks on the door. I was his teacher, the adult, and I could not keep him safe. I cannot keep anything safe.

I put my phone away to talk to my son, who is sorry, so sorry, for making me wait up. He leans on me. I hug him. "We'll talk later," I tell him. I watch him go up the front steps, open the door, clumsily but trying to keep quiet. I stay up. I take my phone back out.

That's when I see the tiger.

My white tiger is on the roof, framed by the power lines and moonlit clouds. He is like an absurdly large weathervane, or a crowning gargoyle. Maybe he was waiting up, watching out for Jacob, too.

Or else he is just enjoying the warm night. He is hunched over, sitting in the company of the gray cat from next door, who is lifting her feet one by one and cleaning them. My tiger absentmindedly mimics this behavior.

I watch them like that for a while, licking their paws in parallel play.

I watch a moment longer, until the gray cat pounces down nimbly onto a nearby fence, then out of sight. My tiger watches intently. He tenses, then lowers himself, as if to jump down and follow the cat.

They say algorithms learn. Maybe my tiger is interpreting this feline outline, mimicking it, learning from the cat, learning how to be something else rather than a memorial, something wild.

I bet he sticks the landing and leaps over the fence and out. Jacob has gone to bed, but I wait up a little longer, for the tiger to make it back, too. I think his territory is growing. But I know he is not gone.

· · ·

The first time it happens is at a grocery store, a few weeks after spotting the tiger on my roof. I feel a tap on my shoulder, tentative and polite.

"Excuse me," says a man. I turn around. I am facing a Black man with a grocery basket full of yogurt. He is wearing bracelets that jangle up and down his wrists and a polo with the logo of the bank down the street. I've never seen him before, I don't think, but he wants to show me something on his phone, is already reaching to hold its screen toward me.

Two tigers stalk the freezer aisle, batting at each other. Mine is the lankier one, by just a little, and has a closer pattern of stripes across his muzzle. Their tails are high as they circle each other, a mixture of wariness and fascination at having found each other.

"Is that yours?" the man asks. He is wary, unsure.

I hesitate.

I hold my phone up, too, and sure enough, see the same scene.

"Yes," I say. I turn my phone to show the man.

The tigers bound between the Push Pops and the Toaster Strudels. A woman unknowingly rushes her cart through them.

We are both smiling, first at the tigers, then at each other. We have a shared mystery, a different layer of reality we carry with us. I set down my basket. We step aside to let the other shoppers through. We watch the tigers till one follows the other around the corner and toward the cereal aisle.

He tells me his name is Bruce. He is the first to lower his phone, and he asks me the same question I will ask others as our tigers keep finding each other in the years that come, the question that I will keep asking myself: "So, who was Dee to you?"

ACKNOWLEDGMENTS

THANK YOU TO my family for your endless support and cheerleading. Special thanks to my mom, Jane Sheffer, my sister, Lauren Sheffer, and the Spitzer family (Debbie, Bruce, Andrew, and Doug) for celebrating every milestone with me.

This book could never have come into being without wonderful childcare for my young daughter: thanks are due to my family as well as the teachers and staff at the Newcomb Children's Center.

To my colleagues, current and former. You inspire me, and your fingerprints are all over these stories.

To the Randolph MFA program and community. I continue to be astounded by the brilliance and generosity of the writers who gather there. To my cohort who committed to the craziness of writing together during the COVID shutdown: David Gloudemans, D.K. Lawhorn, Kelly Sue White, Alisa Otte, Nina Knueven, Ryan Woodard, Matthew Feinstein, Michelle Guerrero Henry, and Corinne Cordasco-Pak. To Gary Dop and Chris Gaumer for bringing us together, and to the incredible mentors who helped shepherd the stories in this collection: Maurice Carlos Ruffin, Anjali Sachdeva, Mira Jacob, Clare Beams, Julia Phillips, John Vercher, Crystal Hana Kim, and Sabrina Orah Mark. Special thanks to Michelle Guerrero Henry, Emilly Prado, and Sayuri Ayers for building community.

To the New Orleans writing community, especially the fine folks at Third Lantern Lit.

To the editors who were early champions of the stories in this collection: Noreen Tomassi, Tina Alberino, Sam Asher, LP Kindred, Lacey N. Dunham, Steve Himmer, Chaelee Dalton, Sheila Williams, Mehrul Bari S. Chowdhury, Joel Hans, Jae Towle Vieira, Aaron Burch, Crow Jonah Norlander, Kalpana Negi, Peter LaBerge, Matilda Lin Berke, Thomas Hobohm, Meredith Morgenstern, Katherine Inskip, and Eric Schlich.

To the Nautilus Writing Group: Amy Johnson, Archita Mittra, Kendra Sims, and Gwen Whiting. Many of these stories began during our initial summer of writing for each other and took shape with your early feedback. Thank you for dreaming new worlds together.

To the many who gave feedback on the earlier versions of these stories, including Danny Cherry Jr., Li Sian Goh, Greta Hayer, and others.

To the Wildcat Writing Group: Corinne Cordasco-Pak and Tierney Oberhammer. I am the luckiest writer because I get to write and chat and workshop with you on the regular. This collection is what it is because of your feedback and support. The things I treasure about you and have learned from you could fill a whole separate book.

Thank you to Jamie Chung for creating the incredible cover image and to Tierney Oberhammer for creatively shepherding that still life into existence.

To the whole team at the University of Iowa Press, including Jim McCoy, Meghan Anderson, Allison Means, Susan Hill Newton, Kimberly Laurel, Karen Copp, Erin Kirk, Maya Torrez, Raj Tawney, and others for the care and hustle in bringing this collection to the world.

To Jamil Jan Kochai: for the surprise of a lifetime, for reading, and for writing the stories in *The Haunting of Hajji Hotak*.

And to Russell—thank you for believing.

NOTES

"Rickey" was originally published in the *Dread Machine*.

"The Unicorn in Captivity" was originally published in *Astrolabe*.

"At the Moment of Condensation" was originally published in the *Pinch*.

"The Observer's Cage," originally published in the *Offing*, is loosely inspired by the discovery of pulsars by Jocelyn Bell Burnell in 1967, for which she was *not* awarded the Nobel Prize. The character of Lizzie is very different from Bell Burnell, in both personality and circumstance. For instance, Bell Burnell was a postgraduate student at the time and not romantically involved with her co-researchers. One of the dangers of writing historical fiction is that the true story is often more interesting than my made-up version. I encourage readers to learn more about Bell Burnell's scientific work and her advocacy for physicists from underrepresented backgrounds.

"Yellow Ball Python" was originally published in *JMWW*.

"The Midden" was originally published in *Necessary Fiction*.

"How We Became Forest Creatures" was originally published in the *Cosmic Background*.

"Reentry" was originally published in *HAD* as "Re-entry."

"*En plein air*" is loosely inspired by the Natchitoches (Louisiana) Art Colony, and the now-renowned self-taught Black painter Clementine Hunter, who, like Josephine, was not a member of the all-white artist colony but began to paint in the 1930s, using discarded paints from the visiting artists. While most of the details of this story are imagined, Hunter was known to portray the daily lives and routines of those living at the colony and to use an imaginative color palette, working within the limits of the colors she could find. She really did use a pink sky in many of her works (see *Flowing River*, for instance). Among other honors, she has been called "the most celebrated of all Southern contemporary painters" ("Clementine Hunter," AAREG).

"The Wedding Table" was originally published in episode 604 in the podcast *Tales to Terrify*.

"Mouse Number Six" was originally published in the *Adroit Journal*.

"The Man in the Banana Trees" was originally published in the *Pinch*.

"The Pantheon of Flavors" was originally published in *Small World City*.

"The Disgrace of the Commodore" was originally published in *Asimov's Science Fiction*.

"Tiger on My Roof" was originally published in *Epiphany*.

THE IOWA SHORT FICTION AWARD AND THE
JOHN SIMMONS SHORT FICTION AWARD WINNERS,
1970–2024